DEMONS AMONG THE STARS

JOANNA KOKOSHKA

EDITED BY

PAMELA SHEPPARD

COVER ARTWORK BY

JOANNA KOKOSHKA

DEMONS AMONG THE STARS
Copyright © 2020 by Joanna Kokoshka

ISBN: 978-1-7351600-3-0

I dedicate this book to those who feel and see the world through the lenses of Autism Spectrum Disorder

∾

TABLE OF CONTENTS

CHAPTER 1

DEMONS AND LIZARDS

Johnny Boy was not having a great day, or a week, or month for that matter. Somehow being a human stuck in a cage in an alien laboratory, full of cages just like his, stacked with others and filled with a multitude of depressed aliens, was not the greatest experience of his life. And his captors? They looked like giant alien lizards. Really, it was just like in those cliché movies— your life just wouldn't be complete without giant lizards. At least the reptiles that captured Johnny came in snazzy suits with military boots.

Who was Johnny? An ordinary human, that's all. A young boy, almost a man who just graduated high school and was enjoying the last lazy summer days before the beginning of the great college experience. What did he look like? An average human, like you'd see if you looked out of your window. Two ears, two legs, two hands, a nose, mouth, dark hair, eyes the color of fire...or beer in case he was sleepy.

If he was missing something, he sure didn't notice it. The girls at his school didn't see anything wrong with him either. Well, all right, maybe he liked those Swedish sugar cookies a bit too much. His mother complained about this weakness of his more than about his messy room.

"You really need to go on a diet." She'd admonish him while meticulously decorating her fridge door with her children's drawings and kitchen magnets.

"You could have been a quarterback on your team."

"Well, I like my position as drummer in the marching band," he'd reply while raiding the pantry for his favorite snacks.

Good memories, now. They kept the only, lonely human alive in this unforgivably alien prison. The bars of most of the cages were glowing and electrified. Those things could give you a hell of a burn. Johnny had learned to sleep curled up in a ball to avoid touching them, even by accident. The lights in this horrible place were always too bright, and like a desert sun left you with no place to hide. The temperature was always hot and humid in this place—good for something cold-blooded like a reptile, but for many creatures, including Johnny, this was a literal hell—too hot, too sweaty, too unbearable. Even the water ration that he was provided daily was hot, almost boiling. Food given to him was in the form of dry and unpleasant waffles.

The alien ship that housed this laboratory was clean. Too clean. It smelled like bleach, and window cleaning fluid unless, of course, some poor alien was getting dissected. Then it smelled like alien guts and agony.

Johnny was not a happy camper. He tried to strike up a friendly conversation with aliens in the neighboring cages but to no avail. The small grey alien creature on one side didn't seem very talkative, and the giant bug on the other didn't have a mouth, just that straw-like structure they used to suck in its nourishment.

There came a day in that alien lab when Johnny realized things were about to change. Well, it was a "day" for lack of a better term, since time seemed to go by differently there, set by the habits and patterns established by the lizards. But let's just say for the sake of convenience that it was a "day" and that on that "day," the alien reptiles seemed quite agitated.

Agitated was a bit of an understatement. One of the leading doctors started spilling his torture, no, 'medical devices,' scattering them on the floor before he ran from the room. The other doctor started furiously doing research, tapping frantically on one of the ship's computers, perhaps using their equivalent of the internet to search answers for something. The doctor kept coming up with nothing, which caused more and more violent outbursts that escalated by the minute.

His assistants were quietly shaking as if they thought something was a terrible idea, but they were too afraid to speak up. Yet, another doctor gecko was constantly pacing in circles. The guards, who usually did most of the heavy lifting and who volunteered daily to subdue and wrestle the feistier aliens just for the hell of it, were unusually quiet and tense. Then, there's the simple fact that practically all of the lizard's moods could be predicted by watching their tails. All of their tails were virtually swishing nervously as if instead of giant reptiles, the room was filled with nervous cats.

This immediately grabbed the attention of everything currently residing in each of the lab cages built by said reptiles. Unlike our Johnny Boy, the alien creatures seemed to know perfectly well what it all meant. Hell, the grey one next to him seemed almost ready to talk. Almost. They seemed to be staring at the main lab entrance with desperation. And hope? Something hung in the air, but it was hard to say what it was.

Soon a group of lizards wearing what looked like hazmat suits appeared at the main entrance. They held laser rifles and seemed ready to use them. Very ready. More than ready. "Like seriously, if one of these guys had dropped their laser, they'd probably die from stress-induced heart attack" sort of ready. Behind them, there were some more reptiles and some more hazmat suits leading in a strange creature in chains. Now that was weird. Johnny remembered that when the reptiles threw him in the lab, chains weren't necessary. He had struggled and fought, but the reptiles and their freakishly firm grips were enough to hold him. From what Johnny could observe in the lab, other aliens were no match for the reptiles, either. What was it about this new and different creature? Now, **this** was interesting.

It wasn't easy to see anything through that crowd of reinforcements. It was a parade of hazmat suits. No, Johnny Boy didn't see anything at first, oh no, no, no. He felt it.

He felt the floor underneath his feet tremble, and other aliens felt it too. It took Johnny a few minutes to realize that this mini earthquake was caused by a growl, a growl so deep it was almost too low for humans to hear. This wasn't a growl of a small creature. Nope, that was the growl of a giant beast. The vibrations first rattled his bones and left him shaking. Then and only then did it reveal itself as a sound. And Johnny Boy soon realized that the thing that at the end of those chains held by those reptiles was making this unholy noise. The caged aliens all seemed ready to say, "I knew it," any minute now. Not yet, but any minute. Some would probably say this with "I knew it" fear and some with awe. But they knew. All aliens, whether they were but an eyeball with legs or some ten feet tall sexy blue dude with antennas on their head. They all knew.

Now, he really had to see this creature, whatever it was.

When this strange procession was close enough, and Johnny could see the growling alien. He couldn't make sense of what he was seeing. He closed his eyes and checked again, and then again, to make sure he hadn't just hit his head and that indeed, this was really happening.

The creature that the reptiles dragged in didn't seem all that scary. Oh, sure, it was a massive creature, and naked. You could easily see it had some muscle to it, but it looked like a human stuck in the middle of a transformation into a werewolf. It was hairless as if shaved of all body hair except for eyebrows. It looked like some mad scientist had tried to help but instead sprouted that sucker with horns all over his head and limbs while leaving the creature's sides and belly extra soft and unprotected. Then to add insult to injury, said the mad scientist had dunked the poor sap in a vat of radioactive green and red paint. Yeah, no kidding. The color of the thing seemed to vibrate. The lizards had green scales too, but they looked positively grey next to whatever the hell that thing in chains was.

And then that thing growled again.

Okay, so Johnny had to admit; the creature was scary when it growled. But when it moved? Well, it didn't seem all that intelligent and seemed comfortable on all fours. It would hop a bit here and there like an overgrown shaved and spiky kangaroo plushy. Why the hell were the reptiles so scared of that thing again?

When the Shaved Kangaroo plushy sometimes stopped and sniffed a particular spot on the floor like a giant overzealous beagle. Ten reptiles holding those chains could pull and pull all they wanted. The plushy didn't even budge. This was quite impressive, actually.

Finally, one other reptile guard brought in what looked like an electric cattle prod and gave Mr. Shaved Plushy a zap. That sure got a reaction, all right. The "plushy" jumped forward on top of one of the reptiles unprotected by a hazmat suit.

The almighty reptile started screaming in pure agony; his hazmat suited brethren pulled the deadly plushy off, but it was too late. A toxic substance on the plushy's skin burned right through any living thing it touched. It sizzled on that reptile's skin, exposing the meat, tendons, and bones beneath. Soon shreds of tissue and skin started falling off the screaming lizard. By the time the scene was over, other reptiles had to use a mop to clean up what was left of their comrade. Meanwhile, the strange plushy decided to stroll by the cages to see all the prisoners.

The creature looked into Johnny Boy's eyes, its red irises, and black sclera calmly taking him in. The beast seemed to recognize him. Johnny thought he could see some kind of emotion on this thing's face, anger, or surprise, amazement, and finally quiet wondering. Pretty impressive. This beast seemed ready to ask something, anything, really. Up close, it just seemed intelligent.

None of the other aliens Johnny had met had ever looked at him with a hint of recognition. How did this monster know humans? This kind of emotion reading stuff was out of the question with other alien species Johnny saw. That was the first clue. The second clue was the fact that the neon plushy had five fingers and five toes. Yeah, true. The five fingers ended in claws and seemed to have paw pads (like you'd find on a dog). But the toes? Those just looked deformed, like they belonged on some ungodly cross between a chimp and a jackal, and two of the toes seemed halfway fused together and looked like a thumb attached to the foot.

But still, there were five of those toes. Johnny never saw an alien with exactly five fingers and five toes. The Reptiles had four, the greys had three, and the bugs had only two—but on the bright side, the bugs had four hands (in addition to their standard-issue two legs). And then there was that squid in a tank. This guy just had a bunch of tentacles. Hell, once Johnny saw an alien with ten fingers. That alien was kind of dead at the time, but the lizards always took stuff like organs and limbs out, not graft them back on.

Then there were the ears. This thing didn't have an outer ear, so its ears were nothing but two horrifically misplaced ear canals, with the left ear situated closer to the top of the head, somewhere near the left eyebrow, and its right ear closer to the right jaw bone.

Okay, so maybe this thing wasn't all that human, after all.

Oh, yeah, the plushy also had a long thick tail, the kind of a long tail you'd find on an alligator. The creature was covered from the bottom to the head in scars like an old elephant seal. Had this thing evolved somewhere on earth? Johnny could definitely picture this creature happily hopping through some earthly jungle in the company of a bunch of cute little frogs.

And so, the strange monster smiled came as close to the human as chains and cage bars allowed, and whispered, "Bye, friend," in a strangely accented English. Though the other aliens didn't hear it, Johnny was still shocked. He heard enough of aliens pleading for their lives in thousands of ways to know that English was not, in fact, the universal language.

But there was no time to enjoy those little inter-galactic reunions. Soon the lizards tightened the chains and pulled the neon plushy away from Johnny's cage. And from the look of things, they were trying to get that plushy into its own cage. Or maybe they were getting ready to execute it. You could never tell with these guys.

The plushy also had another surprise. It was amazingly calm as it stared down the dozen giant reptiles with a dozen laser rifles. The plushy smiled.

And what a smile that was. It seemed to actually purr. The strange creature calmly laid on the floor, like a pedigree pooch would lay down on a rug in front of a fireplace, with his front paws elegantly crossed in front of him. Shaved plushy took in the scenery one last time and then lowered his head, closed his eyes, and died.

Johnny was shocked but had no doubt that the plushy had somehow decided to die, and his body somehow obeyed him. Second of all, Johnny was kind of jealous of the creature. In a place like this, dying when you wanted to die and doing so peacefully without stress seemed like a luxury.

Still, there was no time to get lost in emotions, for the show wasn't over. At first, the body of the plushy seemed to just lay there. Soon it started to rot away, at first slowly, then faster and faster, until all that was left was a skeleton and a pool of green goo. Johnny had never seen a thing like that happen to any other alien species, but he couldn't help but feel elated at the sight. The reptiles would get nothing of value from the plushy.

The final surprise of the day came when Johnny heard a voice in his head.

"Well then, it's over now." The voice said.

"What the hell? Am I hearing things?" Johnny yelped.

"No, it's telepathy, and for the record, I don't appreciate being called a bug-eyed creep." The telepathic voice seemed to come from the giant bug in a cage next to Johnny's. Well, wasn't that just dandy? It appears that the insect remembered that time Johnny tried to strike up that "friendly conversation."

"It's over now?" Johnny asked, turning to face the bug in question, who, for his part, seemed to be fixated on whatever was left of the plushy.

"You don't travel much, do you?" the insect replied. "Okay, I'll try to bring you up to speed then. Telepathy is the universal form of communication in the galaxy. Reptiles are nothing but trouble, and Demons always travel in packs."

"Demons?"

The bug pointed at the bones lying in the puddle of green viscous liquid.

"That's what we call them. Demons. They inhabit a very young galaxy right next to ours. We don't know much about them since they rarely venture outside, but what we do know is that they hate the reptiles. Hell, their skin is covered in poison that only affects the lizards. And since Demons rarely travel alone, that means that soon there's going be a whole pack of them here, a pack that can and will murder every single reptile on this ship. It's over, finally over."

"Should I be scared?" Johnny asked.

"Respectful is a better word; they don't exactly seem to care about creatures other than reptiles. Anyone else would have to really work hard to make them angry. So long as you just let them go back to their asteroids and don't bother them, you'll be fine."

"Their what?"

"Asteroids. They seem to be using those for travel."

"How come they don't freeze or suffocate? I mean, I thought space was a vacuum and all?"

"It is." Another voice joined the mental conversation now, and it belonged to the little gray. "Personally, I suspect that the Demons are much smarter than we think, but since they refuse to communicate, we don't have much in terms of proof. These guys seem to be hell-bent on keeping their secrets."

"Secrets that don't exist," the bug insisted. "They're just animals. Personally, I wouldn't mind keeping one as a pet; they would go great with my house's decor. Sadly, these things never last long in captivity. A few days at most."

"SHUT UP!" This mental voice belonged to a reptile guard who must have overheard Johnny's conversation with the aliens. Trouble was, said aliens weren't scared of him anymore. The gray one especially seemed extra bold.

"Or you'll do what?" The gray was nearly vibrating. "You know you're going to die now, so you can quit pretending you're the boss. It's over now, we won. It's only a matter of time before the Demons will rip you all to shreds!"

The reptile said nothing, only bared his teeth, opened the cage, and grabbed the little gray by the neck. A few hours later, when Johnny saw him, the gray was chained to a medical bed with his stomach ripped open and half his vital organs missing.

How much more time passed was hard to tell. Maybe days or maybe weeks, but things weren't quite the same. The lizards were nervous, rushing around, whispering, hissing.

And then it happened. First, an impact that could either be an earthquake or a direct hit from an asteroid. Johnny shared a look with his neighbor, the bug. No telepathy was needed this time.

The alien lizards shared looks among themselves too. They each armed themselves with laser guns and cattle prods and tried to go about their business as usual. Johnny noticed that every single lizard was armed, even the janitor lizards. Still, it was a time of quiet and slowly rising unbearable tension before a battle could even be heard nearby.

When the time came, the growl literally shook walls. That was the cue for the Lizards in the lab to quit pretending that everything was normal. It was time to join a good fight. They were not eager to battle. Not at all. The reptiles actually looked like they were about to piss themselves. They all lined up next to doors and stood there, sometimes peeking through and then hiding back inside. They were shaking.

The growls were growing stronger. Screams of horror and pain echoed through the halls.

Finally, one of the Demons jumped in like a bolt of lightning, killing and mowing down the lizards left and right. He wasn't great looking, given the bright neon purple and pink skin tone, but judging from his facial expressions, he was having way too much fun killing any reptile in his way. He was practically biting their heads off. This early bird got so careless he almost got himself killed. Almost. He managed to do several backflips and flying kicks before each kill as if showing off. Jumping around like an angry radioactive chimp. Howling like an angry werewolf toying with his prey. Slashing with his claws like a giant tiger. Every now and then, he'd pause and look over his shoulder with pride at the literally captive audience as if he wanted to ask, "Enjoying the show, everyone?" He almost died during his antics when he overlooked one of the guards hidden behind a medical gurney, aiming a laser gun at his back. Lucky for him, his crew wasn't far behind. As soon as they came in, the reptiles collapsed into something of a panic attack and scattered. Yeah, the giant bug had been right. Those Demon things were never alone.

Soon more Demons poured in like a sea of neon-colored killing machines. They came in like a tsunami and did as much damage in an equally short time and left. Meanwhile, that squid guy managed to slip out of his tank, get to the control panel in the middle of the room and to unlock all the cages. Next to Johnny, the giant bug jumped out, grabbed the poor squid, and carried him back to his tank. It seemed that the squid dude barely avoided suffocating. A few other aliens surrounded him and argued about removing the tank and transporting the poor squid guy back home.

Johnny slowly got out of his cage, his muscles shaking from disuse. He stood weakly like he might topple over at any moment. He was free, but possibly a billion light years away from Earth.

The journey was still only beginning. Johnny Boy peeked outside the door and into the hallway. Sadly, the only living things left in this place were the Demons. And there were a few of them, even if the main fight had moved elsewhere.

One old Demon straggler was patrolling the corridors like a crippled tiger. This one even had the white and black stripes just like a cat. Most of its horns were missing, and half of its body looked like it had melted away once and failed to regrow appropriately. None of this seemed to slow down this old beast, as it came close to Johnny in no time.

The creature paused for a second to look into Johnny Boy's eyes. Johnny didn't breathe. The old Demon appeared to be surprised to see a human but snorted derisively and continued with his patrol. Yeah, definitely nothing to see here, people—just a race of aliens who all immediately recognize a human when they see one.

The last time Johnny Boy was on Earth, astronauts had just returned from a Mars mission. No one there claimed to speak with aliens except for conspiracy nuts. So, what the hell was all this about?

Soon all kinds of aliens were pouring into the hallways from their cages and cells. Some were unscathed, some were missing limbs, all were trudging along somewhere. Since Johnny had nothing else to do, he followed them. Sometimes they would come across a stray Demon or two. Some aliens tended to react to Demons the same way humans tended to react to seeing a cute puppy. They'd swarm the creature and pet it, poke it, take videos of it and talk at it. Every now and again, an alien would scavenge something that must have been a small portable tablet from the lizard lab, but instead of using it to call for help, the aliens thought the first order of business was to take pictures with the Demons as if they were some kind of celebrities. Some Demons would show an incredible amount of indifference to all this; they'd continue doing whatever it was they were doing prior to meeting their alien fan club unfazed. But other Demons? They seemed to love the attention they were getting, and they'd pause and act like giant kittens, purring, and leaning in when petted.

Johnny seemed to have nothing else to do but to follow the loud and chittering alien crowd to the reptilian spaceships' landing dock. Different kinds of

Aliens were getting ready to go home. None of those homes could be called Earth.

As he wandered around aimlessly, he stopped near one of those asteroids where the Demons lived. It looked like it had crashed through the ceiling, though luckily, the hole was patched up with whatever pieces of junk that could be found lying around. Two of the Demons slept right in front of the asteroid entrance, unperturbed by the commotion beside them. Both of the monsters had a multitude of fresh cuts seeping a thick dark green liquid. And both of them were purring or growling at something in their sleep, hard to tell either way. With nothing else to do, Johnny decided to approach the two. A sleeping monster wasn't that scary, right?

Sometimes, a human can be his own worst enemy; he tripped over his own two clumsy feet and fell. He didn't get hurt, but he did cause quite a ruckus that echoed in the nearly empty hangar and woke the sleeping beasts.

Their reactions were priceless. First, they sniffed the air, then opened their eyes and noticed him there. They lifted their heads and looked at each other as if they were debating if they should let the stray human in. Finally, one of the monsters stood up on all fours and blocked Johnny's way.

"Hey there." the human greeted them as if he was talking to one of his old buddies from school. "I wanted to know if you could give me a ride back to Earth." The Demon standing in front of Johnny looked like he actually understood what was being said but decided to pretend that he didn't. Instead, it stood up on hind legs like a shaved alien bear, bared his canines, and growled. Johnny backed off.

"That's quite a smile you've got there, my friend," he mumbled.

After several hours of watching masses of aliens leave the place, Johnny's fears were confirmed. None of those aliens would take him home. He grew more and more concerned.

"Hey," he called telepathically to a small group of Grey aliens who were currently trying to get a small reptilian craft to work. "Can you guys help me get back to Earth?"

"Where's Earth?" asked one of the Greys.

"I heard of Earth," piped up another grey. "It's a small planet in the boondocks of the milky way. The civilization there is backward and pretty brutal. I hear that if you crash your spaceship there, humans will catch you and cut you into pieces. We might as well go back into a reptile prison instead."

CHAPTER 2

THE LIFE OF A SPACE DEMON

The spaceship dock was slowly emptying both the spaceships and the aliens, and Johnny was feeling more and more like a sad ghost. At one point, he figured, aw, what the hell, and climbed into one of the smaller reptile space crafts. He first had to clear the body of the dead reptile from the pilot seat. Next, Johnny figured he would have to fly away. But that was easier said than done. If there was one thing that alien and earthly flying machines had in common, it was the existence of too many buttons in the cockpit. What was different was that, quite obviously, the alien buttons weren't labeled in English. After a moment of hesitation, he decided to press a few buttons at random; and hey, he actually managed to start the engines. Encouraged, he pressed a few more buttons. But no such luck this time. Johnny crashed his ship into the nearest wall.

It took a while for Johnny to get out of those scrunched up doors. He wasn't feeling well; he stumbled out of the wreckage and slumped against the wall, sliding down to the cold floor and closed his eyes.

He woke after a few minutes, or hours, and looked around again to the asteroid and its demons. That's when he made his decision. He'd have to sneak onto their ship.

And so, he made his way to the asteroid while trying not to make his intentions obvious. He put his hands in his pockets, he whistled a bit, made a few circles, and was promptly chased away by the demon guards. Those guys were on to him, that was for sure.

So, he hid behind one of the leftover space ships and waited. Soon enough, he saw a monster go in through one of the smaller holes, a side entrance perhaps? With guards distracted and greeting a few other of their brethren, he ran over, slipped in, and quickly was enveloped by near complete darkness. Well, this wasn't a claustrophobic situation at all. He used touch to guide him through what seemed to be and felt like a cave. It was his touch that allowed him to hide in a crevice whenever he heard the monsters approaching. He'd hear them snort, inhale and exhale loudly like a whale, no doubt trying to sniff him out before moving on. And once they moved on, he'd come out of hiding and started following. Where to? He didn't know; he was driven forward by the simple fact that he couldn't turn back.

All good things must come to an end. One of the more suspicious monsters came back with reinforcements, and together they sniffed out our human and used their claws to dig him out of his hiding spot. They grabbed Johnny, not caring if their claws drew blood or left permanent marks. They spoke loudly and angrily in their language, which wasn't telepathic but wasn't English either.

Johnny was too exhausted to show fear or any real instinct for self-preservation. And well, what do you know, apparently giant monsters really hate it when you invade their privacy.

The Demons holding him lifted him off the ground while trying to decide what to do with their stowaway and dragged him through the multitude of corridors. There were dark blurred walls and ceilings and Demon mutterings. It came to a stop only when the Demons came to a stop. And Demons came to a stop in a large chamber, lit by artificial neon lights, with benches, showers, and lockers, and a whole bunch of Demons strolling on two legs in various stages of undress.

Huh, Johnny thought. So, the grey alien was right. Demons were much smarter than they appeared. All of them, a crowd of about sixty or so, now paused whatever they were doing to stare at him.

"Oh, shit," Johnny muttered to himself. "This isn't going to end well."

This wasn't just some series of caverns in an asteroid; it was a spaceship disguised as an asteroid. And the creatures who lived here kept their secrets very well.

Well, so long, cruel world. Johnny felt this was the end. These monsters were going to kill him, or worse. One of Johnny's captors actually yelled something in some of his demon tongues and used a grand hand gesture to call someone over. That, someone, was obviously the head honcho of this place, the king, the emperor, the top dog, the tsar, the president, whatever the hell you want to call it.

This was the guy who was in charge. He wasn't wearing anything fancy, just a simple piece of white fabric draped in such a way to cover as much of the body while avoiding those silly spikes. There was not much to distinguish him; maybe the belt in the middle was a bit more bejeweled and ornate. Sandals on his feet seemed to have touches of gold and diamonds here and there. No, the real thing that made him stand out was how other Demons reacted to him.

They immediately parted like the Red Sea to let him pass. And he? He walked forward with such confidence, so calm and royal, showing off his scars with pride like badges of the highest order. There were a lot of those. Every inch of uncovered flesh told a story of some incredible battle. The fresh wound on his nose was barely stapled together, while underneath it, an older scar offered an explanation as to why part of his lip was missing, giving him a near permanent snarl.

Boss's skin was yellow-goldish in color with a multitude of blue freckles, or were they polka dots? Johnny had never seen any animal on earth with coloring as garish other than those cute little tropical fish in pet shops.

When the Boss finally stopped, Johnny shrank back, feeling that his personal space was being invaded. The guards would not let him go, and if anything, their claws dug deeper. Meanwhile, the big Boss inhaled and forcibly exhaled the air a few times, sounding like a surfacing whale.

If Johnny had to guess, it seemed like the boss was asking for some explanations. And the explanations that came must have been lousy ones since the Boss seemed to get more and more annoyed by the answers he was getting.

When the big Boss finally had had enough, he raised his hand, and the guards fell silent. Growling, he looked at Johnny, red eyes burning with hatred. He raised his claws as if to strike him. But soon, another growl shook the room, and another purple and pink monster pushed in through the crowd. This one parked himself between Johnny and the snarling Boss. More growls and words were exchanged. And then it happened. The purple monster started speaking English. Heavily accented, odd sounding English, but English all the same.

"Quit the bullshit, Xaj'v" the purple one barked derisively at the Boss. "It's obvious that the human has figured us out." At this point, every Demon present gasped in horror.

The purple Demon, Kiv shrugged, unimpressed, and spoke again in that strange unknown language. This time you wouldn't need a translator to figure out that Xaj'v, the boss' response showed he was absolutely livid. The purple one seemed scared too, yet he continued.

"No, I don't think that. I mean, have you seen other humans here? This one seems lost. He probably thought we'd get him home."

Xaj'v snorted, and once again, Johnny didn't need a translator. Apparently, the words, "WE'RE NOT A SPACE TAXI!" are universal across the galaxy. The next sentence, "WE ARE NOT SPACE CHAUFFEURS EITHER," was also universal in any language.

"No, but, well." The defender tried to speak again only to be silenced by Xaj'v, and the rest of the argument was fought in the monsters' native language. Yet it seemed that the monster boss was having trouble persuading everyone, while the defender calmly and repeatedly worked on his case.

Finally, the boss decided to give in, and his next sentence was spoken in English.

"You know the rules, Kiv. We aren't leaving our galaxy, which means that the human will either be killed, have his mind erased, and dropped off at some alien ship, or he'll stay here with us forever!"

The purple one, apparently known as Kiv, also decided to switch to English.

"Maybe we should ask our guest what he wants." Kiv ventured as he laid his eight-inch razor-sharp claws hand gently on Johnny's shoulder.

Johnny nearly jumped out of his skin. He looked around only to see that every monster present was focused on him once again.

"Does he even speak English? They had more than English back on earth!" called a voice from the crowd.

"W-well, I do speak English." Johnny stuttered. "And I... I don't really like any of those options."

There was a bit of laughter in the crowds. Soon a few more Demons came forward and stood between Johnny and Xaj'v, in silent solidarity.

A few voices called out, "Let the human live."

Xaj'v, it seems it was outvoted, and his angry face twisted into a snarl. A snarl was worse than his usual one, anyway.

"It is your idea, Kiv. You will be responsible for the human!" And with that Xaj'v stormed out of the room, snarling all the way furiously.

Johnny suddenly felt weak and dizzy. All the strange things he's been through were finally catching up to him, giving a hell of whiplash and one big concussion. Next to him, Kiv just snorted in laughter.

"So, my tiny intrepid human, you've got a name?"

"It's John..." Johnny's voice tailed off into a whisper as he started to weave back and forth.

"Johnny Boy, huh? Okay then. Say, do you like marshmallows?"

Johnny fainted.

When he came to, he started screaming. He didn't want to but after being captured by space lizards, waking up to see one staring right at him gave the poor guy a bit of a PTSD. This lizard's dazzling smile (filled with razor sharp fangs) didn't help much. Soon really strong and really gentle claws were steadying his shoulders.

"Hush, hush, human. I'm one of the good ones."

"Huh?"

The demon called Kiv stood next to the lizard, chuckling at Johnny's confusion. "Not all the reptiles are bad, you know. See that face tattoo she's got? She's one of the good ones. She's on our side. Now quit screaming."

"Now. You still want those Marshmallows?"

"No, he doesn't!" the lizard lady replied.

What do you know? Johnny could see it was she, after all. Then again, that hazmat suit she was wearing over 90% of her body did not flatter her. Not at all. At least it was a pink hazmat suit.

"What this human needs right now," she continued with the authority of a doctor, "is a small but extremely nutritional meal that will provide strength and hydration without overburdening the gastrointestinal tract!"

"Easy Ł'łяоя. I didn't know you spoke technobabble in human language as well!"

"It's called medical jargon, your knucklehead. And if it's part of my job, then I should speak it fluently in many languages! What kind of a doctor would I be if I didn't?"

"Hl-hloya." It was funny how they pronounced her name. Johnny tried to pronounce it himself and wound up failing miserably. They pronounced the "l's" with their tongues between their teeth, similar to the sound of "the" in English. The "L's" sounded slurred. And also, really, Kiv couldn't understand that? Johnny decided that he had been rescued by an alien idiot. He looked around and could see that he was in a hospital, or was it a med bay? Anyway, he was in a hospital looking place; on a hospital looking bed, next to hospital beds that all were occupied by demons in various amounts of pain. And even though the facility looked extremely futuristic and high tech, there was nothing to relieve the pain in the creatures around him. It seemed that painkillers were an alien concept for those aliens. Worse, Ł'łяоя seemed to be the only one responsible for the wellbeing being of a dozen of these suffering patients. She looked tired, worried, and unhappy with the situation.

"You know," said Johnny, "if it wasn't for those tattoos, you'd be quite cute."

The lizard almost smiled at this.

"Good to know, human, because I took the opportunity while you were passed out and tattooed your face as well."

"WHAT?"

"It's necessary. The tattoos will tell Demons that you're an ally. Otherwise, if they saw you on their home turf, they'd kill you on sight."

Before Johnny could protest some more Ł'ꙗoꙗ shoved a bowl of green goo into his hands.

"Eat up human, it's probably not what they fed you back on Earth, but it should give you strength."

The green goo smelled like food. Johnny looked from Kiv to the Doctor."

"So, do you drink this? Eat this? Slurp? Is there a spoon somewhere? A fork maybe? A chopstick or two?"

But the two friendly aliens ignored his questions. They didn't seem interested in any instructions. So, Johnny brought the bowl to his lips and tried to slurp this weird mixture of green water, green cornflakes, and nose snot mixed together. The good news was that unlike the dry food he was forced to eat until now, this thing actually had some taste to it. The bad news was that it tasted fucking awful. Our lonely human Johnny was seized by a vicious cough as he choked on the foul-tasting stuff. He spat out whatever disgusting goo was in his mouth.

Ł'łяоя, for her part, wasn't angry or insulted. "I guess this was still too heavy on your stomach. Don't move. I should have something much lighter somewhere in here."

Meanwhile, Kiv was snickering like an immature teenager. As the tattooed, hazmat-clad, and otherwise lovely lizard nurse turned around and marched to the other room seeking something that was supposedly better to eat, Kiv picked up what looked like a sack and took out a small bag of marshmallows.

"Here ya go, my intrepid pet," said the gentle monster while offering Johnny the sweet confections. "It'll help the medicine go down." And with that, he turned and hurried out of the hospital room.

A few hours later, and after figuring out how to eat alien food without throwing up, Johnny was released from the hospital bay. As he stumbled along in the corridors without any ideas as to where he was going, he caught up with the nearest bunch of demons who were engaged in some riveting conversation. With nothing better to do, he followed them. They all noticed him but otherwise ignored his presence. One demon gave an approving nod and said, "nice tattoos."

After a while, they rounded a corner and were back in the control room. Xaj'v was there too, though he didn't seem to notice Johnny. Or maybe he did and didn't want to notice him.

Without the whole "I'm gonna die soon" thing hanging over his head, Johnny could look around and admire the place. It was impressive. There were no windows, but a multitude of cameras provided a panoramic view of the outside on screens. The control room itself looked like the coolest cave ever, outfitted with strange and complicated technology. A multitude of chairs, control panels, workbenches, and plenty of giant monsters monitoring everything. Add to this a constant chatter of a hundred voices speaking in that bizarre language.

Still, there were some things that gave Johnny an emotional jolt. Coming across, Johnny saw a Demon who looked just like the green and red Demon, who died in the reptilian lab that fateful day. The beast in question noticed the shocked human and managed to quickly figure things out.

"So, I guess you did meet my brother, huh? He sure was a hell of a fighter, but we can't let the reptiles find out what we're made of." The beast trailed off as Johnny watched several expressions cross the beast's face.

"Anyways, my name's Jakj'mer. I'm sure you're dying to find out what we're doing here, right?"

Johnny did manage to nod his head; yes, and for Jakj'mer, that was all that was needed.

"Well, it's very simple: we're waiting for everyone to leave. Once that's done, we'll go back home as well. Sadly, it will take a while.

"Yeah, whenever we aren't fighting, our lives are quite boring. But on the bright side of things, that means that you should get used to things rather quickly!"

Oh great, that's precisely what Johnny always wanted. To be stuck on an alien ship full of bored aliens. Jakj'mer seemed to be quite good at reading emotions though and offered Johnny an empty seat next to his.

"Let me guess, human: you don't really know what to do with yourself now, right? Well, I'm sorry to tell you, but there isn't much to do right now; most of us are just talking to make it seem like we're important."

And that was true. For some reason, Demons were using the same twelve-hour system to measure time, which meant that Johnny got to witness each excruciating minute that was passing by. And they had an oddly similar writing style, too. Watching the nearest screen, Johnny saw a bunch of letters that looked just like the ones from the human alphabet.

Something was strange in this place, he thought. Was he dreaming? At this point, dreaming seemed like the most logical explanation.

Worse yet, Johnny felt a strange urge to ask about more things. His logical mind kept reminding him how seeking the things that seemed familiar had backfired in the most spectacular ways during the last few hours.

Conflict and the constant bizarro feeling of deja vu mixed with some Venetian carnival freak show was building up beneath the surface.

Soon enough, Kiv showed up, this time with a box of chocolate cookies. "Would our intrepid human care for a cookie?" Because, of course, he would. Jakj'mer was less than amused.

"If my keyboard stops functioning because of those crumbs again, I swear I will kill you!" He warned, but Kiv just laughed.

"You'll have to catch me first!" For the second time that day, a sweet snack was shoved into Johnny's hand.

"Cookies are good for everything!"

"Kiv, I'd seriously appreciate it if you could refrain from corrupting our newest team member!"

"Do you mean our intrepid human? Jackie, didn't you know that corrupting the innocent was truly the most fun thing to do?"

"And for the last time, do not call me Jackie."

"Easy there, Jackie. If you glare at the monitor screen any harder, it might explode!"

Yup. It's official. Johnny owed his life to an alien clown. Jakj'mer let out a deep, long-suffering sigh before turning to the human next to him.

"You see who I have to work with?"

Johnny was too young to have worked anywhere other than as a fast food restaurant drive-through operator. He was ambitious, but a combination of a bad economy and alien abduction had put a temporary stop to his educational plans. Still, he tried to be helpful and came up with a solution that seemed perfectly reasonable to him.

"Why don't you complain to the manager about it?" This apparently was complete bullshit from the point of view of an alien space-demon, given the exasperated look that appeared on Jakj'mer's face and Kiv's side-splitting laughter.

"Kiv's the second-best fighter we've got. Which means he's practically untouchable," Jakj'mer explained.

"And then there's the little detail of our "manager" being none other than Xaj'v, you know, the dude who tried to kill you? And who practically made you a prisoner on our ship?"

Johnny backed off, thinking: **okay, so this wasn't maybe my brightest moment, but I am kind of out of my element here**. Not knowing what else to do, Johnny decided that now was a perfect time to munch on his cookie. It seemed like a good strategy because once the laughter died, it was followed by a minute or two of uneasy silence between the three of them. Then Jakj'mer ended this moment of silence was by screaming as loud as he could:"M'jąδ'δąhяa! Meяa! oξyfя!"

Johnny almost fell out of his chair. Kiv cracked up, laughing again and knowing that there would be questions.

He translated: "Looks like all caged aliens left. Jackie sounded the official alarms. Once it is established that no one can witness our departure, it's time for us to be on our way."

"Why all the secrecy?" Johnny asked, but this time it's was Jackie who answered:

"What they don't know can and will kill them—and we're kind of in the business of killing stuff."

Their departure did not happen immediately. Demons were checking, re-checking, and re-re-checking that the alien docks were cleared of all aliens. It reminded Johnny of a wait at some DMV offices. Soon he fell asleep. When he woke up, they were already in space.

Kiv, being Kiv, explained exactly how, during Johnny's nap, their entire spaceship was teleported into outer space.

"Dammit. I would have liked to see that." Johnny cursed to have missed it.

Johnny Boy had no choice but to become fast friends with the Demons. Mostly because there was no one else. Soon he knew not just Kiv but also his crew. They were about two dozen strong. The main players were G'juat, the beast with the unique green-white-brown skin pattern and about half of his horns missing, Kȟod, whose name Johnny couldn't pronounce if his life depended on it. A few other guys were united by one thing. They all admired Kiv for his physical and battle prowess, though not so much for his brains. Turns out, everyone on the ship knew Kiv was a well-meaning clown. The good news, though, was that he was relatively easy-going, easy to talk to, and if he had a bad idea, you could easily correct him (unless your name was Jakj'mer and you tried to prevent Kiv from wrecking your computer). None the less, his battle status gave him some measure of respect, and that respect meant that his team wouldn't harm their new pet human. This couldn't be said about Xaj'v and those who supported him.

This was another reason for Johnny to learn to recognize his alien roommates and fast. Granted Xaj'v and his crew wouldn't kill him, but they did slam him into the nearest wall a few times simply because he stood in their way.

Yeah, when these guys decided that they would allow him to live, it meant that he needed to live at least 10 feet away from them at all times. And that was just the tip of the iceberg.

Kiv was hell bent on showing off the whole ship to Johnny as if he was the one who created it. He showed off the training gymnasiums, the swimming pool. This was where Johnny discovered that none of the Demons could swim. They all seemed to love water anyway. (Inflatable floating devices and spiky monsters do not mix). Kiv showed off the library and a few other insanity inducing places. He showed off the main hall where the monsters ate their lunch. The food was all right. What it sorely lacked in the meat department it did make up in the bug department. Fried tarantulas, roasted silkworm pupas, mealworms, and scorpions dipped in chocolate provided a main source of protein. When asked about it, Kiv, who was practically bouncing off the walls at this point, explained that it is easier to grow plants and insects. So easy, in fact, that they were growing their own food right on the ship. Standard meat, on the other hand, always came from the supplies picked up planet side. Johnny soon found out that such meat almost always involved something distantly related to spam in one way or another. Spam, spam, spam everywhere. After a few weeks, he came to accept spam as something that, well, it existed.

And then there was Ł'łяоя́а, the lizard. Johnny tried to make friends with her, too. Here, there was less of a problem. Łip, as she was nicknamed (thank God, the shorter version was a bit easier to pronounce) tended to be very easy going, all things considered, and Johnny did like to come to the medical bay where she spent most of her time anyway. No emergencies needed. This was mostly because whenever she wasn't patching up Demons, she'd still find an excuse to stay to scrub the medical tools, clean for the hundredth time, disinfect the floors, and take stock of all the available medicine time and time again. She actually slept on one of the medical gurneys. She even set up a nice heating lamp and a lawn chair in one corner and a target in another, all so that she could sun herself and throw a few knives whenever she wanted to relax. She amused herself throwing anything sharp and pointed. Knives, scalpels, scissors. Łip hit the center of the target every time.

Johnny only wished someone had told him that before he was almost accidentally stabbed. Not knowing what else to do and trying to avoid getting squished by accident or, otherwise, he wound up spending a lot of his time with Łip and even started practicing knife throwing. Ł'łяояа, for her part, seemed to understand that a human mind needed something to do and calmly accepted a new companion in her life.

Life with aliens on an alien spaceship was surprisingly boring for Johnny. The comet spaceship they inhabited was a patrol ship called Kohutek. It circled the distant outer edges of the galaxy, and whenever it found a spacecraft belonging to another alien race, the job of the crew was to make sure that the aliens never found out about the Demons. When they ran afoul of the Lizards, then they would simply slaughter them. Still, there were a few surprises.

One morning Johnny was awakened by alarms blaring and a smell of burning. The whole spaceship was shaking. He thought he was going to die any minute.

"What's going on?" He coughed and stumbled out of his cabin, only to be nearly run over by Demons. Of course, Kiv had immediately volunteered to be the tour guide and grabbed the human by the shoulders while excitedly yelling over the ship's alarms, "SNEAK ATTACK!" He then let go, ripped off the toga he was wearing, and jumped into the ranks of his comrades, who like him were stripping naked and removing all the signs of technology or culture, from watches to cell phones.

Soon enough, Kohutek crashed through the roof of the Reptilian ship, and the experience was exactly as pleasant as it sounded. The asteroid jolted and shuddered. Demons held on to whatever was nearby to steady them. Johnny was thrown from floor to wall to ceiling.

The landing was even more pleasant. As soon as it was over, Johnny ran into the nearest bathroom and puked whatever he had had for dinner last night.

The alarms finally quit screaming; the silence a small thing that made life worth living. Once his ears stopped buzzing, Johnny decided to join his friends. He ran, stumbling through the hallways until he somehow managed to slip into the main hall where Xaj'v stood as naked as the day he was born. Xaj'v was in the middle of giving an important speech to his crew.

Jakj'mer caught Johnny and sat him on the nearest bench.

"My friend, I hope to God you're not thinking about fighting." He looked worried.

Johnny didn't know what he was thinking, but he did manage to notice a thing or two.

"You, you're wearing cl... clothes? Nobody else is."

"I am the ship's navigator and the spotter. I do not leave my position. I can fight if I must. I am merely more useful here."

"So, it's a fight?"

"Yes, now come, my friend. I have the best view of the action." The best view of the action was indeed, the control center, where Jackie's beloved main computer was situated. And on the giant screens, one could easily see the hallways of the lizard spaceship. They saw the fear in the reptilian guards' eyes, and soon one could feel the growl of the demons.

"Heh, our troops are getting ready to rip them to pieces." Jakj'mer beamed, then stopped, realizing that his human may not have known what he meant.

"We growl whenever we go into battle. It is our battle cry, well, battle growl."

They watched the screens as the space lizards started firing their laser guns toward the Demon spaceship wedged in the side of their ship, temporarily cutting off the visual feed with flashes of the blasts and smoke. Then as suddenly as the shooting started, it stopped. The lizards watched in silence. Had their efforts achieved anything?

Nope. Soon enough, growling vibrated again, this time stronger than ever. This time they could see the reptiles starting to shake. Some threw their laser rifles on the ground and started running. A few smarter ones ran away with their rifles just in case they needed to try to defend themselves.

And then it started. Demons jumped out of the ship. First down was Kiv, and he effortlessly avoided blaster rifle fire. A few jumps here, a few jumps there. Green blood flowed, where a few laser blasts grazed his arm.

"Our blood has a really high concentration of biliverdin." Jakj'mer knew there would be questions, and he didn't mind being a tour guide. "Biliverdin is the green pigment; in humans, it shows up in bruises and is the reason why people with jaundice look strange. The reason why we have so much of it is that it is poisonous at this concentration. It is just one more reason for our enemies to fear us."

That's when Johnny realized Demons had a ban on telling him about anything about themselves. Yet, Jakj' mer was doing precisely that. He looked around. He and Jackie were the only ones in the control center. Everyone else was getting ready for a battle.

Ł'łяояa came by and stood beside them. She gave Jackie a silent look of understanding, then glued her eyes back to the screen where Kiv was doing his usual dance, trying to get the lizards to accidentally shoot each other.

"That's not the only poison at their disposal," she added. "We need our environment temperatures to be really high in order to function. Demons do not, so they start sweating in high heat to cool off. The sweat also has a highly effective poison in it geared specifically to kill my kind."

Yeah. This explained why she was still in her hazmat suit. At this point, Johnny was starting to suspect that she had physically fused to it.

Soon the whole team of Demons jumped out of the ship and started the slaughter. That's what it was: a slaughter. The lizards didn't stand a single chance and were mowed down.

Sadly, when the battle moved down the hall and out of camera range, Johnny was left to guess how the battle continued. He did hear plenty of screams that sounded quite lizard-like. And cheers of joy when captive aliens were freed from the laboratories.

"Well, I guess I should head back to the hospital now," said Łip. She was about to turn towards the nearest exit when Johnny stopped her:

"Why do Lizards keep aliens in laboratories?"

Łip thought a while before answering. "For the same reason anyone would. For their genes." Johnny watched as Łip turned away abruptly. He saw the strange look on her face, but it was too late to ask and too late to apologize for his question.

"And for the future," Jakj'mer added just as Łip retreated, "Do not ask our Doc about the lizards. She was raised among us, so she knows as much about those space geckos as we do."

Training drills on the Kohutek were scheduled on a regular basis. Demons would assemble in the gymnasium and train for a few hours every morning. No humans and no lizards were allowed to participate. Ever. Johnny would come to sit in the bleachers and watch the event. He kept coming even after that time when one Demon was thrown during a fight and landed on top of him. And the time another Demon was stabbed and that vicious green blood splattered on top of him and left him horribly burned. Or the times when he was accidentally hit in the head with a medicine ball, and a chair, and a table, and a moped. Okay. Just why in the hell would Demons need a moped? They could run faster on their own!

"As you can see, my intrepid human pet," Kiv helpfully explained while Johnny was lying in a hospital bed hooked up to various pieces of alien machinery for the umpteenth time.

"Our technology allows us to repair spinal cord injuries, including broken necks and concussions way better and faster than anything you humans ever invented! In fact, we know more about the gray matter than the Gray aliens themselves!"

Which was fortunate because Johnny Boy was in there precisely because of those injuries. Actually, the human managed to get acquainted with various types of demon healing technology quite well over the past few weeks, and yes, it was generally speaking quite advanced. But less fortunately, Kiv was being his obnoxious proud self again.

Johnny, in a desperate bid to shut him up, figured he should find an awkward question to do the trick.

"So, if you guys have all of this advanced healing technology," he started, "why is it that you never use any painkillers? Not even a simple numbing agent?"

Kiv did become oddly silent for a second when he heard the question. He looked about to make sure no one was listening and leaned in, whispering, "Those would kill us."

That almost explained things. Or not? Were all Demons allergic or something?

Whenever Johnny thought he could start relaxing, his peace would be interrupted. Either Xaj'v o one of his crew would show up, and Johnny Boy either had to find the nearest exit or press himself against the nearest wall and hope he wasn't noticed. These guys could and would push him around just because no one would stop them.

Soon Johnny was familiar with how everything on the ship worked. The spacecraft flew around the edges of the Demon's galaxy and mercilessly killed all the reptile aliens occupying any planet or satellite. Mornings, such as they were in space, involved breakfast, gym training, weapons training, and a few other trainings. Then came lunch, and after lunch, some rest and relaxation until supper. Sometimes instead of supper, there was an attack on the giant lizards.

Łip often worked overtime to patch up the crew. She didn't hesitate; she didn't seem to have second thoughts. No one seemed to be questioning her, either. Until one day when Xaj'v was busy brooding and looking all-menacing, Ł'łяoяa came by and shoved a tablet with an important looking list with a bunch of red letters shining from it.

"Well, hello to you too, sunshine," Xaj'v said by way of greeting.

"Cut the crap, boss," the lizard lady barked. "We need those supplies, or else I'll have nothing left to patch up the crew with. I've sent you the e-mails about this. Why haven't you replied?"

"We have to get the job done f..."

"...after we buy the supplies. Send e-mail to the elders if you have to. They can replace us for a week!"

"Not if we want a spot as top warriors in our galaxy."

"That can wait until next year."

"Next year? Next year? Every year is the next year! We are always in the top ten spots, but we never win!"

"And there's nothing wrong with that," Łip said. "We are quite important to the war effort, and you know that. Unless, of course, you're trying to prove something. Something that has nothing to do with us winning. Something, like some useless test tube..."

At that Xaj'v suddenly exploded with a growl so harsh that everyone and every living thing seemed to shrink in fear.

Everyone except Ł'ɫяояа.

Xaj'v did not like to listen, but Łip was stubborn. She smiled pleasantly before continuing.

"If you want to win anything, give your crew a rest. They've been in space for ten months now. You're not going to win the best fighter award, but it's not too late to try for the most compassionate leader of the year award!"

Xaj'v relented. Soon they docked at the nearest planet.

CHAPTER 3

TINY PLANET AND THE BIG TRUTH

The planet in question was called "Mali яасяа." Johnny was told that it lived up to its name, which would have been useful if he knew what "Mali яасяа" meant. It turned out to be a small planet situated near the edge of the galaxy they patrolled. It had plenty of forests, from the frosty ones near the poles to the tropical ones near its equator, and all other kinds of forests in between. There was plenty of water, though less than on earth. The crew landed in a city, the only city on the planet. Everything else was small villages and termites. Sadly, local termites had not yet reached the self-awareness stage of evolution, let alone a willingness to trade anything.

Speaking of cities, this one didn't look at all futuristic. The biggest and only city of the Mali яасяа planet looked as if the building were stolen from some Victorian earth town. Their numerous arches and pointed windows, not to mention random towers aplenty, looked out of place. And just like the demons themselves, those buildings were painted an array of gaudy and vibrant colors. The cobblestone streets were made out of giant jewel stones that sparkled in the sun. Street lamps stood tall, elevated on poles, so ornate they almost defeated the purpose of a street lamp in the first place.

Johnny thought for a second that he'd accidentally walked into Disneyland park. But no, it seems this place was actually inhabited. Turns out that yes, the city had all the modern and futuristic technology. But the city itself just didn't look as futuristic as Johnny expected.

As the ship landed, the elder demons who ruled the city and the entire planet came out for a greeting. The six of them looked like they had all been through hell and back. Scars on top of scars, some missing eyes, and several missing limbs. There wasn't a single elder that could be described as "whole." They arrived without fanfare.

A few curious demon kids stood by at a safe distance before being shushed away by their (also battle-crippled) nannies. With the sight of young demons, Johnny Boy finally got his answer to how demon mothers managed to give birth to their prickly bundles of joy. Apparently, Demons grew horns later, possibly at puberty.

But Demons weren't the only ones who were there to greet them. Robots were there too, though not at first. Soon one curious robot stuck his head around the corner.

Another robot carrying some heavy luggage dropped everything, called other ships' friends over to join the elders and meet the new guests. Those monster kids with robot babysitters had the pleasure of greeting new arrivals instead of being told that they should carry on with their normal lives. And then some other robots joined in, and then some more and more again. Before long, the crew was surrounded by a mob of curious machines. The Demons were celebrities and appeared to enjoy the attention from the robots.

Other inhabitants of the city were the lizard aliens. They looked like they'd all be related to Łip more than to their war-like, likely slaughtered, friends. Dressed rather modestly and all sporting those ugly face tattoos, their reactions were a nice mix of Demon-like disinterest and robot-like wonder. Some would gather to greet the new arrivals, but the others would just shrug and keep their distance. They didn't seem as prone to hugging anyone as much as the robots were. In fact, it seemed like a good many of those space geckos had scars on them, burn scars. They seemed to be preoccupied with their mundane, boring old jobs and raising their families full of tiny new space geckos. Even the little ones were already tattooed. One thing for sure, even if they weren't as numerous as robots, they actually did seem to outnumber the Demons living in the city. They didn't seem to bother anyone here, nor did anyone bother them. Not at first glance.Soon the other elders arrived, the oldest and most battle-scarred Demons who effectively ruled the city. They seemed amused by the commotion. The space ship crew bowed respectfully; greetings were exchanged.

One of the leaders approached our hapless human. The beast was battered and had seen better days. One of its eyes looked as if it had been gouged out with a blunt fork. Half its tail was missing, and a bad limp slowed his walk. Nevertheless, he stood tall and proud and even managed a good-natured smile.

"So, this is our tiny trouble maker, huh?" The aged beast looked Johnny over. "A human, how sweet. What do they call you?"

"J-Johnny...Sir"

"Johnny. Well then, nice to meet you, Johnny. I am I'itiяa, and here are our other council members: Kü'üяa, Яапяa, Zukяa, Усжяa, and Ψусяa. We make the rules for everyone here. We hope you will follow and respect our laws, and in exchange, we will make your stay here as enjoyable as possible." With that, he went back to Xaj'v, who seemed less than pleased by the interlude. Johnny could tell he was angry, probably because the elder spent time greeting him first. Though Johnny had to admit it was rather funny seeing the king of beasts standing aside and being snubbed like that.

Staying on Mali яасяа was indeed quite enjoyable. Most of this enjoyability took the silvery metallic forms of robots scuttling about. As Johnny watched those lively crowds, he noticed a strange thing. There were robot artists, robot bakers, robot singers, robot social workers, robot tourists, robot film makers, robot janitors, robot teachers, and robot movie stars. There were even a few robot chefs at what appeared to be a five-star restaurant. The food they made was inedible for machines but was much appreciated by every Demon in the city. They had jobs and money to spend. And spend it they did. There were shops galore, and robot babies were left to have fun in the streets, sometimes joined by the Demon kids. Such a strange thing to observe. They seemed so different from other conscious robots in the galaxy, so happy and carefree, pursuing lives of pleasure and creativity.

Johnny looked at everything with a strange fascination. So many things about the city looked familiar, but Johnny didn't know why. His curiosity did not go unnoticed. G'juat caught him staring on more than few occasions. The usually shy monster had a slightly devious smile on its face.

One evening while loading fresh supplies onto their Comet spaceship, G'juat told his friends to go on without him and moved over to Johnny, who as always was considered too weak to do anything useful and thus was left by the wayside to admire the spaceship airport.

"You want to make new friends?" That was oddly brave of the big, shy beast.

"I think I already have plenty of friends."

"But how many of them are robots?" G'juat knew he had won by now and didn't waste any time taking advantage of this fact. "An old robot buddy of mine happens to be in town. Tonight at 8 pm we're going out to this little bar. It sells a good beer for us and a great oil for the robots. Wanna join?"

"Might as well." Johnny had nothing to do, after all.

Johnny found his way to the bar to discover that G'juat and his robot girlfriend and her robot family were already there. His girlfriend was obviously the "old robot buddy in town."

The place was rather nice, all things considered, though the number of robots definitely outnumbered the number of Demons. G'juat's girlfriend was called Pip and was quite a cheerful creature. By now, Johnny wouldn't have expected anything else. Really. She insisted their human sit on a chair she saved for him, right between her and her robot parents Tip and Zip.

When the beverages were brought in, the questioning began.

"What was earth like?"

"What was the school on earth like? And food? And work? And fashion? And love affairs?"

And thousands of things that Johnny may or may not have known about, though he did get choked up when it came to talking about his family.

"There was nothing very special about us." Johnny stopped, remembering. "We are average people living in an average house not too big, not too small. My sis is probably still trying to get into art school, and my little brother is probably dreaming of becoming a mad scientist. Grandma and Grandpa live right next door. Man, I wish I could still be there with them."

G'juat seemed to be almost offended at that.

"What's the deal here? We don't torture you. We show you everything, give you food, and still, you mistrust us?"

"I don't mistrust you," Johnny mumbled. "I just want to go home."

"Well, you seem to be rather ungrateful then!" G'juat countered. "We could have easily killed you! You know how secrecy is important to us! And yet, we..."

"Honey, that's enough." Pip cut in. "He's not a warrior like you. He is likely to think differently about things."

"No, no, no." G'juat had said more in the past five minutes than he had in the past few months. He still wasn't done yet.

"This kid has been a prisoner on a reptile ship. He saw what we're fighting and why we're fighting it. This ungrateful little bastard should know why we do what we do!"

"Sweetie, please!" Pip cut in again. "You are a warrior, so a fight will be most important to you, but he's just a human. The family must matter quite a bit to him as well. I know, to me, it does matter a lot."

A few more minutes and G'juat was fully placated though not completely done with staring daggers at the human. Though awkwardness that reigned in those moments, Zip figured that this was a perfect moment to change the subject.

"So, Johnny Boy," he started. "I take it you were wondering about us robots then, huh?"

"Well, yes... I mean, back on Earth, we just started developing artificial intelligence, and I've got to say we haven't quite figured it out just yet."

"Hah! So old humans made some progress after all!" He was cut off by G'juat's glare. Still, without missing a beat, he explained, "Well, our existence is simple enough. With so much time away fighting, Demons needed help raising their kids and keeping their cities up and running. So, they made us."

"Yes." Tip chimed in. "After a while, we developed self-awareness and became fully functioning members of society."

"Just like that?" Johnny was surprised. "No fighting? No anger? You were just given a citizen status?"

"There were some debates," said Zip. "But the elders and the wise were quick to point out that if we were to be treated as slaves, that would inevitably lead to revolt."

"We have been treated as equals ever since we've proven that we could handle it."

"Better than that, really," added Pip. "We don't have to fight; we get to pursue our passions, so long as we stay within the bounds of our galaxy."

"So that's really it? No taboos or anything?"

G' just stared intently into his beer, reverting to his old quiet and subdued self. "Well, there is one taboo." He sighed. G'juat noted while reverting to his old quiet and subdued self and staring rather intently at his beer. "It is still frowned upon if a robot and demon marry."

The next one to invite Johnny to a family reunion was Kȟod. Luckily for our human, this time there were no crazy family secrets revealed, or anything unusual. Just a typical monster family in a typical monster house. Kȟod's wife was off fighting in the war in another spaceship with another team. Kȟod himself rarely got to visit their six kids, who were being raised by their grandparents. Grandparents who were all retired warriors of various ranks and had the scars and medals to prove it. Not much more to say here. It was an evening of domestic bliss with a family celebrating the unexpected yet welcome visit from their father. That evening, behind the fence in another family's garden, a few neighbor's kids sprawled on the fresh cut grass looking at the stars above them, searching quietly for their parents.

Jakj'mer's family lived far away, somewhere in the center of the galaxy. He didn't seem to mind, though. He decided that once planetside, he would spend his time gathering up as much of the spare tech as he could find. This wasn't much on a tiny planet known for its scenic views. There were no giant factories. The newest tech wasn't available.

Jackie decided to buy as many spare computers and portable hard drives as possible, even if they weren't up to date. He wasn't keen on having a human help him in this endeavor, either. He wasn't rude about this, but he did question the idea rather strongly.

"You know nothing about our tech, Johnny. Your weak human muscles are nothing compared to our carrying power. And you actually want to help?"

"I want to be useful."

Jackie begrudgingly took our human shopping with him and then let him carry some of the boxes. Nothing too heavy, nothing important, but Jackie was right; he wasn't much help. He couldn't keep up. It didn't help that Jackie had a naturally fast pace. Walking back to the ship that day boiled down to a very exasperated Demon stopping every five minutes to wait for his human companion to catch up to him. After about an hour of this dance Jakj'mer simply laid down the bags he was carrying and ordered his human to do the same. They hitchhiked their way back to their spaceship, catching a vehicle big enough to load all they carried as well as themselves. The day ended with Johnny apologizing for his inability to help. Jakj'mer merely sighed and smiled sadly, then said

"You should go hang out with Kiv; you know?"

"Yeah, well. Kiv disappeared."

"Yeah, that's the usual problem. Kiv tends to disappear whenever we dock."

"And nobody cares about this?"

"He shows up on time whenever we leave to fight. In the grand scheme of things, that's all that matters."

There was a moment of silence that allowed Jakj'mer to briefly look around the control room as if to figure out where to store all the stuff they bought.

"So that's all that matters? Fighting? And where do I fit?"

"Do you really want to know, or are you just asking?"

"I sure as hell want to know. I want to know everything. And I hope you're not like G'juat, are you?"

"Not at all."

"Good! Why the fuck did he get angry at me? I simply said that I want to go back to my family. What the hell? And I want answers. I want all the answers in the galaxy!"

Of course, Johnny's anger attracted attention, though conveniently, the attention was only from Łip and her brand-new medical supplies.

"Ahh, the sudden, unexpected burst of anger." She mused out loud while inviting herself into the group.

"All my literature on mental health did point out that it would happen sooner or later."

"What the hell are you doing here?" The human barked more harshly than he intended.

"You want answers? Great. The curious mind can win many battles, but the first answer is that we were all explicitly forbidden from explaining things to you."

"What?"

Seeing that against his better judgment, their human was ready to strike, Jackie decided to butt in.

"Xaj'v did. The only way to change this rule would be for you to plead your case to him."

Johnny blanched. "Couldn't I ask Kiv? Could he do that for me?"

Łip and Jakj'mer shared a look, and our human again felt like a small child in a room full of adults. Jakj'mer smiled sadly before replying.

"The relationship Kiv has with Xaj'v has been getting worse and worse since you've arrived. The time Kiv showed you the whole space ship? He wasn't supposed to do that, nor was he allowed to show you our training sessions, or translate our language, or do anything for that matter."

"So, he won't help me?"

Łip actually snorted at that. "Oh, he'd help you, and that's the problem. If he tries to help you, Xaj'v will try to rip his head off."

Jackie pulled out a chair right next to Johnny before adding his two cents worth. "Best case scenario, Kiv, and Xaj'v challenge each other to an official duel. Kiv gets lucky, wins, and takes over the leadership here." The Demon paused for a second. "But even then, the majority of our crew prefers Xaj'v's leadership. That would guarantee further dissension and weaken our team. Not a great thing in our line of work."

Łip took this moment as her cue to show her maternal instincts.

"You should perhaps stay planetside and wait for another team to pick you up. It would be the safest option."

"Would another team let me go home?" Johnny asked.

The silence that followed was deafening, Łip was quiet and looked away. Jakj'mer did not hesitate. "Human, your wish is illegal, and as long as you're in Demon galaxy, you always will be. But we have on our ship someone who could help you and perhaps limit the bloodshed to a minimum. J'juk'кея."

J'juk'кея was an enigma ever since Johnny met her. She was the Demon with the black and white stripes arranged in the same pattern as those of a lion fish. Females of the Demon species were as strong and as large as males. They had no breasts unless they've just given birth, either. The only identifying external difference was skin color. Females had striking black and white patterns; many resembled markings of sea snakes or milk frogs. Some even resembled certain species of butterflies or caterpillars. And the insides of their mouths were pastel blue in color. Just like males, each female had the dual combo of venomous blood and venomous sweat as her main weapon.

J'juk'keя was old, so old in fact that Johnny always wondered if she would be allowed to retire soon. Another peculiar thing about her was that she seemed to be the team's pariah, but why, Johnny couldn't quite tell. He never saw her do anything illegal, yet she seemed to be shunned by Xaj'v and his followers and, to some extent, by Kiv and his group as well. Even stranger was the fact that despite her age, J'juk'keя seemed to be one hell of a fighter. In the beginning, Johnny contemplated approaching her and talking with her but was warned not to do so by one of the demons.

No explanations, just a stern, "leave her, or you'll join her." And now it was made relatively clear that he should talk to her after all, despite all the previous warnings. And he should probably to do so when other Demons weren't going to see him.

So, he did just that.

It was by accident that Johnny discovered her hideout. She was staying near the river that cut the city in two, right underneath the bridge. She had a tent, and a small fireplace, even a clothesline with freshly washed clothes drying on it. The place looked oddly clean.

J'juk'keя must have spent a few hours every day sweeping then washing stones on the beach, at least that's what it looked like. Of course, if she would have kicked out the giant termites that had set up a nest nearby, it would have been nicer. Much nicer. Those things were the size of dogs.

Speaking of the she-devil herself, she didn't seem angry about Johnny's sudden friendliness. She was quietly resigned to it. She did immediately notice that Johnny was trying to sneak on to her turf, though. There was an awkward minute or two as Johnny tried to remain calm as he approached the old monster sitting by the river. What would he even say to her?

'Hi, my name's Johnny, pleased to meet ya. By the way, I only wanna be friends with ya because I hear you could help me break the law. Whadda ya say?'

Yeah? Um, no. That that wasn't going to end well, he just knew it. Still, not knowing what to say or how to say it, Johnny simply sat down next to the old warrior and stared at the water flowing by. The river was so calm, full of frogs and birds and fish that you'd swear that this wasn't a different planet but some exotic location back on Earth. It was too bad that all those little creatures couldn't help our human talk to the monster sitting just two feet from him.

Finally, it was J'juk'keя who broke the awkward silence:

"Let me guess. You wanna go home." She barked so brusquely that Johnny nearly jumped out of his skin.

"...and you want me to help you." Not even a question, this old lady knew what was up.

"Will, will you do that?" Johnny asked.

"Maybe," she snorted. "Meet me here tomorrow at sunset for your test."

"Wait, what? What test?" This did not sound good.

"Before I decide if I can help you, I'll need to find out something first."

And with that, she was gone.

That evening Pip the robot decided to show Johnny around town. They saw the sights, pretty and exciting, but Johnny wanted to find out a bit more about Pip herself.

"So, what do you do for a living?"

"Oh, I'm a bartender at that oil shop down the street; I'm really lucky, too. They pay well, and the customers are respectable, too, not like that shop on the other side of town. Most importantly, it is a stable job. My sister's job? She's got this weird idea that one day she'll be a movie star and moved to that big planet at the center of the galaxy. And now, what? She keeps begging us for money!"

"That's really, um, normal. Why don't Demons live like this?"

Pip deflated somewhat upon hearing this question but did her best to answer.

"They, they have to fight."

"Why's that? Do you robots force them to fight?"

"No, of course not! They.,. They just have to... to fight."

Johnny could tell that this particular conversation would go nowhere, so instead, he decided to ask Pip about the unusual buildings around him. Pip, of course, was more than ready to chatter on.

"Well, you know we have had several awesome architects come through and build some really amazing buildings, which you wouldn't have guessed. It's such a small planet, after all."

That's how the rest of the evening went. Still, every now and again, Johnny would see a few Demons out and about, most of them either really old and retired or really young and almost ready to leave for their military training. They did a weird thing with their phones where they'd bump them together. Johnny asked Pip about it, and the robot girl laughed somewhat nervously at the question:

"They are just checking to see if they're related," she explained. Pip was obviously embarrassed.

"We each have our entire genealogical tree written up in every piece of electronics we own. That way, if our datapad or phone connects with that of a stranger, it can calculate if we are long lost cousins. Demons tend to use it all the time in order to find out if they're related, because, well. Let's just say that there's been a genetic bottleneck that nearly wiped them out. There were less than a thousand of them left once. So yeah, they need to do this all the time if they go on a date to avoid accidentally dating their long lost cousin."

The next evening found Johnny under the bridge by the river waiting patiently for J'juk'keя to come. It was quiet as the animal species traded shifts. Nocturnal species took over the posts of diurnal creatures. As soon as the blue sun of the little blue planet started to set J'juk'keя showed up, decorated in the last rays of the day. She wore a simple tunic tied up with a rope belt in the middle with a rather sorry looking sack slung over her shoulder. She greeted him without a single word. She gave Johnny a quick nod of her head, and they were off.

They followed the river upstream away from the city and up into the mountains until they finally reached a small cliff near a small and noisy waterfall. The sun had almost completely disappeared beyond the horizon now, and with so many trees around, darkness enveloped them fast.

J'juk'keя calmly climbed up on the nearest boulder. Johnny decided to sit on a fallen log nearby. The monster seemed to be a queen of silence, perfectly comfortable with long stretches of it. Here the waterfall was the only one roaring. J'juk'keя calmly, almost lazily, pulled out a datapad from out of her sack, then quietly wrote something on it, and handed before handing it to Johnny. The electric pad shone brightly. The words written on its screen formed a simple question: **What do you know about human technology and space travel?**

"What an odd question," Johnny thought.

Then again, everything about these monsters was odd. He took the pad and wrote down, "**Well, I know that we landed on the moon in 1969.**" He passed it over to J'juk'кея. She read it and cracked half a smile.

With a quiet sadness, she wrote a reply: "**What if I told you that space exploration started a century before?**

Now Johnny didn't need to say or write anything. His confusion was visible. J'juk'кея simply wrote down another sentence. When Johnny read it, his blood turned to ice.

A secret human society started in 1869, where those of us who were most oppressed gathered with one dream. To get away from this wretched earthly planet and find a new home among the stars. Over time we became demons."

It all made sense. He didn't want to believe it. Yet it made sense. He couldn't breathe. He thought he might pass out. But J'juk'кея. She was there. Ah. So that was the test, wasn't it? To see if he could handle the truth?

Well, he could.

Did it work? He wrote the question with shaky fingers. **What do you think?**

And so, for the next few days, J'juk'кея simply told Johnny the truth he craved for so long while she silently judged and assessed his every reaction.

And the truth was relatively simple, yet horrifying.

The Demons were once humans.

Humans managed to get their funding for their space trip from a multitude of illegal operations back on Earth. Those humans created spaceships full of plants and animals like tiny arks and left Earth searching for a better home, only to find out that all the best homes were already taken by aliens. This presented a major problem, especially if back on Earth, you had made a living selling illegal drugs, weapons, and kittens.

They were considered criminals; unwanted. With that kind of record, no one would be happy to see them again.

And so those humans were stuck. Stuck in space. Not welcomed on Earth. And then came the lizards, a race of aliens so violent and deadly that nobody dared to oppose them.

The beauty of being a part of a small group was that you could be accidentally wiped out by the dumbest thing imaginable. It wasn't that the lizards had some kind of vendetta against humans the first time they met. Simply speaking, when those lizards tell you to move, you move: if you don't, they'll blast your ship into oblivion.

For the space geckos that was Tuesday... or Monday, or whatever.

For the humans, early in their travels, that was the day half of their fleet was wiped out. What the lizards didn't know back then was that they had created their own greatest enemy.

Humans eventually did find a galaxy to make their own. It was small and only very recently formed. Most of its billions and billions of planets were still hot and unstable and fresh out of the oven. They used whatever was left of their earthly menagerie to seed life wherever it could be sown.

"All those trees here," 'J'juk'кея pointed at the forest around them. "All came from Earth."

She looked off to the horizon. "All of the creatures here, they used to live on earth, too. We set them free here and let them live as they pleased."

But that was not the end of the story. Humans used the genes of some of the animals they brought in to modify themselves into better fighting machines. They needed to defend themselves against the lizards. Their experiments came with side effects, of course.

"Dogs like pugs that were bred with flat faces, they can't breathe and can't smell. When we tried to give ourselves an enhanced sense of smell, we'd have to make room for it. Our genetic modifications couldn't stop there.

We gave ourselves super-traits from all the species, like the snake's heat sensing ability, or the bird's ability to see ultra-violet light, or those long canines so that whenever we fight, we don't automatically lose a tooth. All those modifications had to have room to fit."

It was scary to listen to this, but J'juk'keя had pictures to back up her claims. Her datapad had videos to show. Videos from the many, many laboratories, from the many, many doctors and scientists who researched and recorded everything over many, many generations. Everything was explained.

The bizarre ears? Demons wanted to be able to discern not only if a sound was coming from left or right. They wanted to know if it was coming from above or below as well.

Poisonous skin? Claws? Spikes? Increased muscle strength? Useful for fighting, obviously. Prehensile feet? Improved climbing ability. Bizarre gender dimorphism? Demons wanted to prevent their enemies from knowing who was who. And so on, and so on.

Each and every single modification had a consequence. Heavy muscling, increased bone density, and little to no body fat meant that no Demon was a natural-born swimmer. Yet they still loved the water, and so another change was added, nostrils that could close and open on command like those of a dolphin, and lungs that could last fifteen minutes so that way even if a demon couldn't swim, it wouldn't immediately drown. Those mutations caused other accidental consequences, like the fact that now they were officially conscious breathers and had to command their lungs to take each breath as if you command your hand to pick up things or punch something.

Simple things like anesthesia became a death sentence, and many more died on operating tables. Some Demons died in their sleep simply because they couldn't tell their lungs to breathe. So, they added a few dolphin genes, the ones that allowed their brains to sleep one half at the time. Now, while one half of their brain was resting, the other was awake. After a while, they would switch.

Their spines had a unique structure borrowed from a tiny earthly hero, a shrew, making them capable of lifting something ten times their own weight. Such modifications had a side effect of making their spines incredibly inflexible, and suddenly they now needed a tail to balance themselves, especially when walking on two legs. But that also had side effects, and so new changes had to be added.

Large claws? Another problem. Now the changes were piling on without an end in sight. And so on, and so on, until the demons were no longer human.

"And by the way, that's how we got our growl," J'juk'keя said one morning while washing up in the river.

"Growl?"

"Yeah, you know, the growl, the thing where we snarl like a wild animal and the vibrations can shatter walls. That was an accident. By now, nobody knows which genes were responsible exactly, just that one day we could growl."

J'juk'кeя never hid anything from Johnny. She was strict, as well, unlike Łip, who always accepted his presence, as she did for all of the others.

"Go spend time with others. You'll be ripped to shreds if someone figures out you've been talking to me."

Speaking of Łip, now that she was surrounded by robots, she shed her hazmat suit in favor of a simple gown, with a piece of cord for a belt. These days she occupied her time writing e-mails to her friends, sipping lemonade, writing postcards, reading up on the latest scientific developments, and then writing some more.

When she saw the stricken look on Johnny's face, she knew immediately who he'd been talking to. She knew he needed a distraction, needed to get his mind off the truths that weighed him down. But she also knew of every knife -throwing competition in town and so was more than happy to take Johnny along.

Ł'łяояa could get over-zealous at these competitions. She had a knack for throwing sharp objects and managed to win more than a few times. She also liked to complain about the food served at these outings.

"Seriously, I know that most of the inhabitants of this planet are robots," she muttered in annoyance. "But when they serve organic food, could they at least give us other choices than hamburgers and hot-dogs? What the hell? You can't stay in tip-top shape eating this crap!"

"Says the lady who constantly drinks lemonade!" Snickered Johnny, finally back to his old self.

Yes, this giant lizard, who seemed to be unfazed by just about anything, could lose her cool at the mention of junk food. Who knew? But that brought up another question.

"Why aren't you allowed to fight?"

Ł'łяояа visibly deflated at the question and answered quietly. "It's against the rules."

Again, in a subdued tone, "it's against the rules."

By now, Johnny knew to leave it alone. Ł'łяояа gave him a few more "happy pills" as an apology. They proved very useful.

Johnny also hung out with Kħod, the laid back family man who had a whole list of attractions lined up for him, from going to the cinema to various amusement parks. He was used to taking care of six kids, so he didn't mind a seventh one tagging along. One evening at the city fair, Johnny noticed Kiv, sitting on his own in a Ferris wheel boat eating cotton candy and looking out to the city. He had such a pensive, quiet look on his face; he was almost unrecognizable.

Kħod decided to invite Johnny to one more party, his daughter's graduation from middle school. It was a ridiculously big party, like a bar mitzvah and sweet sixteen combined, and a multitude of guests, not to mention a live mariachi band. Kħod's eldest was done with school, which for her meant joining the military.

To prepare for that, she would go off to meditate for six months in one of the planet's many vipassana meditation centers. At the end of the party, she and her other classmates were to take a vow of silence, not to be broken for the next half a year. She would be in the company of other girls and kept away from boys, forced to eat a vegan diet while meditating in complete silence for twelve hours every day. After that, it was straight to the military school and then off to the war.

Wait. Why were they celebrating? This didn't sound like a happy event.

When asked about it, she and her whole family kept insisting that this was just the way things were.

"We might be the best killing machines in the galaxy," she explained. "But we always know that only half of our children will come back from war."

"But don't you want to be something, anything else? Like a musician or a doctor or a... a janitor?"

"But I can be."

"Really?"

"If I survive the war, I can retire and be whatever I want."

"OK. But what about before that?"

"I'm a fighter."

"Do you have to be that before you retire?"

"I'm not a human," she said. "And I'm not a robot either."

"And your brothers and sister?"

"They are fighters too."

There were never any questions there—only conviction. Then, as if taken by a sudden bout of pity for her human guest, she added, "Don't worry. At least my father is here for the celebration. Not every Demon is this lucky."

That same night Pip invited Johnny to yet another party, her cousin's sweet sixteen, to be precise. And what a difference it was! A simple coming of age party. No talk of a crazy long separation, no vows of silence, and no going off to war. Just a happy family having fun.

"So, what's with the secrecy?" Asked Johnny the next day. J'juk'keя didn't seem to react at first, but her answer made sense to him when she did.

"Well, think, human. Do you really think that modifying yourself into what appears to be a monster is looked upon kindly in this galaxy?"

"I guess not."

"Well, there you go. Other alien races, they use genetic modifications to eliminate diseases. We use genetic modification to turn ourselves into killing machines. Who would want to make friends with a killing machine? Personally, I believe that the only reason we weren't busted yet is because of what lizards are doing. We were doing everyone else a big favor. They had managed to piss off all of their neighbors. So, when we decided to devote our lives to exterminating them, other alien governments must have decided to look the other way."

"And you would kill everyone who decides to rat on you?"

"I wouldn't, but I don't make the rules. I tried to tell aliens what we were once, and I've paid the price."

She looked at Johnny pointedly. "Happy now?"

"So how will I get back to my family?"

J'juk'keя smiled at this.

"Simple," she said.

"We'll be back in space soon enough, fighting. And during those fights, a clumsy little human could get lost and killed. That's when you could find a spaceship and fly back home."

"But I don't know how."

"You'll learn, kid," J'juk'keя reassured him. "You'll learn."

With that reassurance, Johnny felt he could ask one last question.

"And what about Kiv?"

"What about him?"

"Why did he disappear? Do you know?"

"I know everyone's secrets, but I also know that Kiv would have to tell you himself what's going on."

And so, the stay at Mali яасяа came to an end. The Kohutek was restocked with supplies, Demons were well rested, and Kiv, as always, showed up at the last minute, just in time for the journey. This time, since there was no reason to disguise itself; the spaceship simply took off like a helicopter instead of teleporting.

It was a wonderful feeling. Johnny knew now that he had a secret ally who would help him get back to Earth. The roar of the spaceship engine never felt so good.

CHAPTER 4

VERY GRUMPY, COSMIC FAIRY GODMOTHER

If there's one thing no one seems to talk about flying in a spaceship, it's how cramped it can be, especially after a week planet-side. Though it was still bigger and better than what any Earth humans ever built, the constant smell of sweat seemed to seep everywhere, and it could drive someone crazy. There were routines to go back to as well.

Keeping Kiv company was one of them. It was easy to see why Kiv was such a prankster. Life could get tedious if your only mission was killing space lizards. But drawing dicks on your napping friend's face was more impressive when your friend was indeed a monster that was never fully asleep. When asked how he managed to do this Kiv simply shrugged and said, "Years of practice!"

Yes, a lot of things seemed more impressive now. Like that time when Kiv managed to sneak into the dining hall and switch everyone's maple syrup with soy sauce. But there were some demons you should never prank.

One day everyone saw Kiv running through the ship with a very furious, and very wet, and very naked Jakj'mer hot on his heels.

"Let me guess," Johnny said to Łip who stood next to him clad once again in her signature hazmat suit.

"Kiv tried to switch Jackie's toga with lingerie while he was in the shower, right?"

"Yup, and if I know anything about those two, either one or both of them will end up in my med bay in about fifteen minutes." Łip nodded and tried to hide a hint of a smile.

Still, some of Kiv's ideas could be bizarre. Johnny witnessed Kiv and G'juat fighting together using staplers and staple guns for fun. And yes, they were picking of staples off themselves for days afterward. Both of them thought it was hilarious.

"Why do you guys have staple guns anyway? You have no paper; you use data pads all the time." Johnny asked.

Kiv shrugged: "We stole them from Med Bay. That's how we stitch up wounds."

But normalcy, such as it was, tended to be interrupted now. Johnny soon found out where J'juk'keя resided. He found her in the engine room. Technically, there were security cameras everywhere on the ship, and in there too, but J'juk'keя had a few tricks up her sleeve to make it seem like no one would ever visit her. What kind of tricks? She wouldn't tell. But no one seemed to bother Johnny much about his visits. By now she had taken it upon herself to become Johnny's teacher. The hum of the engine would block any sounds of their conversations that could have been picked up by the security devices.

It seemed that this old girl could make a spaceship out of a shoebox and a paperclip. Her main idea was not so much a spaceship but a mecha-suit for her human student.

When Johnny asked why she simply said, "You can remove your face tattoos, you can try to hide, but our men will come after you and try and kill you. You'll need something to be evenly matched, and I doubt your human family would want to welcome back their genetically modified human son."

"Will Kiv come after me too?"

"I don't know."

And so it went. But J'juk'keя? She wasn't done yet. Not by a long shot.

"You wanna get out of here? You've got to learn our language!"

"Why?"

"Because everyone assumes you don't know it, so and each time they say something important, they'll switch back to our language. Let's be honest. What you don't know can and will kill you."

And so once again, our human would find himself holding conversations with a Demon using a data pad to communicate while a spaceship engine was roaring in the background. The data pad had written on it a list of letters read the same in The Demon and English language: "A B D E F G H S M N T U V W O P R I J K L Z."

"That's a lot of letters, And they're exactly the same as English?"

"Not really, R is a rolled one, but if you say it the English way... you'll be understood, most of the time."

"Okay, what's next?"

"Letters that are somewhat English: G is always read as in Gravity. Y always read as "y" in Syllable or "i" in a bit. Then there's C Q and X. We read those as clicks. # is not a hashtag; it's our guttural "H." Be careful. Наяа means lover but #аяа is bastard; only one letter difference there. Ü - which we borrowed from German and read the same way. Ŧ read as "th." Ł read kind of like a mixture of "th" and "L" kind of a "hl." Then we have letters with accents: Ć Ś Ñ Ź. The closest English equivalent for those would be "Chi," and "She," and "nye," and maybe "si" in Asia and Vision."

"Wait, what? Why can't you just write it as "Chi" and "She" instead of Ć and Ś?"

"Where would be the fun in that? Besides, we haven't gotten to letters borrowed from Cyrillic yet."

"Cy... what now?"

"Cyrillic, the Russian alphabet. Here are the signs we borrowed from them: Ж, Я, we read those same as Russia does. And we have this sign, П but we read it entirely differently. You're supposed to bark like a seal when you read it.

Ћ came from Serbia and is read the same way. We borrowed these signs too: Ѧ, Ѫ, Ѭ and we read them the same way Russians do, or the way they would if they still used them."

"Slow down! That's insane! Who needs these many signs in an alphabet?!"

"Just be happy you're not learning Chinese."

"Anything else I need to learn? A few signs for pixie dust, maybe? A letter to spell the names of Greek gods with?"

"Well, since you've asked, we borrowed a few letters from the Greek alphabet as well, human, though the Greeks would have a field day if they knew how much we Demons tend to butcher them.

Here they are: the Δ, the delta in Greek, the Dzelta in ours, the Ξ, xi in Greek, the gbi in ours, Ψ, the Psi in Greek, the sha in ours."

"Oh, fuck my life. Are there more?"

"Well, actually there are, but for now, I don't want to scare you off, you sad little human. We'll leave it there."

The next meeting with J'juk'keя was less frustrating. She decided it was time to try on the mecha-suit and test it for glitches. It was a closely fitting sort of thing. What was it made of? Johnny couldn't tell. A sort of metal, maybe, but light and flexible. The suit was clunky-looking, like those special effects from old black and white movies.

Johnny was a foot taller in it. And it was awesome.

"First, do simple things, like walking around in it." J'juk'keя sounded like a cranky space godmother. Walking around, he felt a little weird, a little bit lighter than air, floating like that. J'juk'keя simply pointed at a random block of cement she had propped up in the engine room.

"Punch it!" She ordered.

Johnny punched it as hard as he could. The cement broke easily. This was amazing! Finally, he felt like he could do something!

Old J'juk'keя, for her part, just scowled.

"Ay, human. Your stance was horrible! You've obviously never trained to fight, have you?"

"Who cares?" asked Johnny. "This suit is awesome!"

He kicked one of the cement blocks up in the air, and with another kick, he smashed it into pieces. He never felt so powerful in his entire life. For the first time in a long while, he felt like he could write his own story instead of just being a passive observer.

J'juk'keя was somewhat less pleased.

"We are all born to fight," she snarled, "but we still need to train, and it looks like you'll have to as well, suit or no suit!"

Johnny didn't mind. It was fun, not just because the suit made it easy, but also because it was something to do. J'juk'keя made sure he had a perfect stance all the way through. And now he could do a hundred pushups without feeling the burn.

The times when they were sparring, punch, kick, left hook, Johnny felt a new sense of power and less fear. It was just so good to be able to do something without having to worry about an accidental stabbing.

Then again, even with the suit on, J'juk'keя could still knock him a few feet back with just one punch. But now Johnny could pick himself back up, dust himself off, and go right back to sparring instead of to the hospital bay.

Somehow J'juk'keя still managed to work him hard enough to make him sweat. She wanted to see everything he could do. Could he jump in this thing? Could he climb walls? Could he crawl? How about swimming? And always, she'd complain about how his stance wasn't perfect and how he was two seconds away from crippling himself.

After each training session, as Johnny was taking off his mecha-suit piece by piece, she'd sit next to him, datapad in hand, analyzing the newest training session. Next time he'd come by, he'd find J'juk'keя tinkering with the suit, trying to improve it.

There were other discoveries. J'juk'keя had other functions on the ship. Whenever a monster wanted something illegal, they'd go to her, for Mausжψħ that was booze. Now Mausжψħ was on Xaj'v's team, so Johnny hid underneath the nearest engine where the beast wouldn't reach him. Still, he didn't need to worry; the big lug didn't even notice. And as for booze, it was allowed on the ship, but in quantities that were never enough to enable you to get drunk.

Mausжψħ wanted more, and J'juk'keя? She'd help out if you asked nicely. She'd still refuse to smile, though.

Still, nothing escaped her sharp eye. As soon as Mausжψħ left, she walked by the engine where Johnny was hidden and practically barked at him.:

"You can get out now, human."

Johnny obeyed. He knew arguing with J'juk'keя was a bad idea.

She even anticipated his question before he asked.

"Nobody's paying me for it. I'm the outcast, so it's assumed I deal with these kinds of things."

Johnny didn't know how to feel at that statement. Maybe sadness. Before he could have said anything, he was blindsided by the flash of J'juk'keя's fury.

"I don't need your sympathy!"

Now, if this had been a movie, he'd have something nice to say. Something that carried a great deal of wisdom that could extinguish even the angriest flames. But this wasn't a movie, and Johnny honestly didn't know what to say. He did the only thing that he thought he could do, change the subject, and check how their little project was doing.

"How's my mecha-suit coming along?" It was the right move as her anger was gone in an instant.

"Your suit will come." J'juk'keя snorted. "Now, we need to practice our language lesson."

Ah, yes. The language. The Demon language was infuriating. The only easy thing about it was writing. The language was written as it sounded. If there was ever a double letter somewhere, it was pronounced as a stutter - the "k's" & "j's" in J'juk'keя's name, for example.

That was it for the easy part. The rest of it, it was so challenging that Johnny would have been ready to skip those rules altogether. But he couldn't, not with grumpy old Demoness pariah breathing down his neck. Suffice to say, he hated every complicated and nonsensical rule that found itself in this hellish dialect.

He started to make some fun discoveries. For one, demon names weren't just some random sounds; they actually had meanings.

K̄hod's name literally meant either hero or husband. Ł'ꞁꞁояa simply translated into compassion, and Jakj'mer meant fighter, which was odd considering that the guy practically never left the ship.

Xaj'v was proving himself to be a hell of a guy, too. He kept calling Johnny "zadaśяa" which translated to garbage.

Speaking of Xaj'v and Kiv; their names were similar now that he knew the language. Xaj meant number Ten while Ki meant seventy-five. He was intrigued and asked J'juk'keя about it.

"You're not too far from the truth, human," she replied.

"When we add a "v" at the end of the noun, it's an equative declension: a way we mark the word as being equal to something. We also use it as your ordinal forms, so Xaj'v means tenth one, and Kiv means seventy fifth."

"Why would they have numbers instead of names?!" Johnny was somewhat outraged.

"Well, they were made by the same mad scientist, both of them." J'juk'keя shrugged.

Seriously, why was he even be surprised at this point?

"Why are you staring at me like that?"

"Anything else I should know? Any more dark secrets? What's next? I'll find out that you guys eat little children?"

"Calm down, little human. You should know by now that we like our secrets."

There were plenty of other things the language said about the demon culture. For example, the nouns they used to describe body parts and machine parts were exactly the same. They'd never use terms like "baby" or "daddy" as a way to describe their lover. Apparently, stories where a child and a parent literally formed a couple have happened often enough that Demons did not find it funny or sweet. The monsters didn't have words to describe the concept of left or right in order to navigate. They just used compass directions, as in, turn north then turn east. Sometimes they'd use expressions, turn towards the heart or turn away from the heart to give directions.

Either that or they were just annoyed that Johnny couldn't tell which way is north.

The language had three genders, male, female, and neutral. Nearly every word, noun, adjective, or verb could be altered to fit any of those three categories.

G'juat liked to use the gender-neutral version more often than not. Johnny asked J'juk'кея, and she simply shrugged,

"G'juat's intersex." She said it as if it was the most normal thing in the universe.

"Everyone from planet Ñoяa is. They modified themselves genetically add genetic variety to our species."

At this point, Johnny didn't even ask for further explanations.

Once Johnny managed to master combat in the mecha-suit, J'juk'keя started slowly teaching him about different kinds of spaceships, how they were built and how to fly them. Some used fuel, and others that used anti-gravitation devices. Many other types using some strange propulsion devices he didn't recognize and which he couldn't comprehend. She taught him with great detail which crafts were preferred by which alien races.

When she saw Johnny staring at her slack-jawed, she shrugged her shoulders and said simply, "Well, it's common knowledge for us, human."

Most importantly, she taught him how to assemble his own starship from spare parts. Step by step. When it came to spaceships, Johnny had to admit that they were fun to admire but a pain in the ass to build. There were different kinds of ships used in different situations. He couldn't remember what those were if he tried. He hardly knew one from another.

Soon a day came when all the knowledge was to be put to the test.

J'juk'keя simply told Johnny, "You're going on a field trip."

"Huh?"

Before he knew it, he was in the spaceship he had made, flying through space and testing out his new ride. The joy was hard to describe. He felt he could fly home right then. He looked around and saw he had no provisions with him. He had to turn back to Kohutek.

J'juk'keя was a fairy space godmother, all right. A very grumpy space godmother but a space godmother nevertheless.

CHAPTER 5

HANGING OUT
WITH ALIENS

Flying around in his own mini spaceship was exhilarating. Even more so because it was fucking illegal. It involved a fair amount of sneaking around. Demons had several docking bays for the smaller crafts to enter and dock. And most of the smaller vessels in question were, in fact, evacuation pods. Of those docking bays, Johnny chooses the smallest one, the least used as his base of operations.

J'juk'keя taught him how to deal with Demon technology, including hacking and tampering with the security footage, but Johnny had a feeling that it wouldn't matter here. His Docking Bay 5 had become a sort of like a garage where the Demons kept all the random stuff that they didn't need, still wanted to keep, but didn't want to get rid of either. The place was basically a dusty old garbage pile, and Johnny couldn't see if any of the security cameras worked. It even smelled like an old garage combined with a dusty attic.

That was where Johnny kept his very own hand-made spaceship. It was smaller and sleeker than the escape pods. The Demon's escape pods were all shaped like broken up pieces of a comet, the better to disguise them. His spaceship looked like, well, a spaceship.

He could fly around the edges of their galaxy and sometimes right into other neighboring galaxies. The aliens, they wouldn't care, and the Demons didn't either. Those aliens never caused the demons problems, so they gave each other a wide berth. Johnny loved flying and took his ship out every chance he could find.

He explored so many of those alien planets. It was like one of those old futuristic human movies, and not surprising. Some of the planets had towering buildings that obscured the sun during daylight hours and plenty of sky cars buzzing about. They were noisy, filthy, and glorious. There he could see plenty of old faces that he easily recognized from those god-forsaken reptilian laboratories, the greys, the giant bugs, and a few new faces like humanoid pigs.

Johnny flew from one forbidden planet to the next. He didn't talk to anybody. He made no friends, yet he was content with walking down their streets and observing other aliens. He tried to remember was that they all liked to communicate telepathically. He learned to keep his thoughts buried and undetectable. But still, at least he didn't need to learn another stupid language.

Even though he was clearly a human, no one seemed to notice him. No one gave him trouble either. Strange, since he never ever saw any other humans anywhere. Then again, he often saw at least one alien in each of the cities whose species couldn't be immediately recognized and who seemed to be the only one of his kind on the planet. So, he felt he would not be noticed either.

Every time he got back from his excursions, J'juk'keя insisted that he'd get in the habit of checking his spacecraft for any damage that might need repair. Same with mecha-suit maintenance. She was like a drill sergeant insisting that her charge develop good habits, except that she was a drill sergeant who could rip him apart with her claws.

As he got more confident flying into alien territories, he started to have some fun on their planets. He tried all the strange drinks, got into drunken fights, and had fun.

And what great fights those were. With the mecha-suit and his new strength, he was no longer confined to the sidelines. Every single punch and kick thrown was thrilling. Punch! Kick! Uppercut! Roundhouse! Hammer's fist!

Oh, how great it was to hear his blood pumping!

Johnny chanted to himself as he fought. **Groin kick! Sidekick! Backhand! Wait, is backhand a fighting move or not? Aw, who cares! Victory yell! Make sure that they hear you in Canada! Well, wherever Canada may be right now.**

Another change came each time Kohutek crash-landed into a lizard lab. Watching Demons fight their nemesis was more fun now. No going home early. Johnny now could fully enjoy the show and comment on the fight unfolding before him. If Jackie and Łip had any complaints, they didn't voice them.

Johnny was about to discover that there were some fights he would not be able to win on his own. How did it start? Hard to tell precisely which alien bar. Alien alcohol was involved.

Well, it was one of Johnny's favorite bars, a little hole in the wall filled with grey aliens where he had to be careful not to bump his head on the ceiling. A place that didn't really sell alcohol, but it sold something alien that tasted like alcohol, smelled like alcohol, and could get you drunk like alcohol. It looked oddly radioactive. Johnny was okay with that. The place smelled bad and half-rotten and had a fantastic old video game feel to it.

Because the greys were prone to being greys, they gossiped a lot. Listening to their thoughts was like accidentally tuning in to some weird old radio station. On one of those excursions, when the ever bored alien bartender nodded to his human guest and served up his usual, this human guest wound up tuning in to one of those outlandish conversations.

This one went somewhat like this:

"Ya, remember those Demons? Word has it they accidentally killed one of the head honchos of the reptiles. Now the lizards are pissed; they're assembling an army to officially strike and kill off those weird mutants. They are ready to wipe them out!"

"Huh, that should be interesting!"

"I'd place my bets on the Demons to win!"

"Nah, the lizards will win. These mother fuckers always win!"

"It'd be a shame to see Demons get wiped out, bud."

"Who cares? It's obvious that Demons are the result of some illegal genetic experiments. If it wasn't for the space geckos, they'd be sitting in jail!"

"Well, at least they could do us all a favor and kill of all the lizards first before they get annihilated."

Hearing this, Johnny couldn't help himself. He launched himself onto the pair. How other alien hell hounds got involved in that fight was anyone's guess. Then again, it's a bit hard to figure out when a hell hound throws you out the window and tries to rip your heart out. Soon more and more aliens started to join the fray, and our intrepid human finally discovered the limit of his battle suit: about 10 greys, 15 giant mantis aliens, and one squid guy. Windows were broken, and things started to look bad when suddenly, a growl shook the ground beneath them. The ground started shaking, and everyone turned toward the sound. And everyone and everything froze. Everyone knew what that meant, but no one could quite believe it.

"A Demon here?" The stray thought floated by.

And all the heads turned. Kiv had arrived. Like a bright purple lion, he strode down the street. No thoughts were coming from him - just waves of pure anger. Pure anger directed at Johnny. All the aliens fled immediately and just in time because Kiv jumped up and pinned Johnny to the ground. He was snarling.

Johnny was dizzy with shock. Man, those canines are big when viewed up close. Once he recovered, Johnny figured he would test out his mecha-suit and caught Kiv with a sucker punch to the jaw. Kiv flew back and landed in the nearest trash pile. The first thing he did was he brought his paw to his face, massaging the spot he'd been hit. His face showed his shock.

As Johnny got back up to his feet, Kiv flipped onto all fours. Johnny was prepared for a fight and was a bit surprised to see that Kiv simply stood there calmly as if judging the situation. After what felt like an eternity, he slowly started circling Johnny as if circling his prey. Careful, calm, silent, and calculating. Johnny had enough of this waiting and attacked first.

He'd heard a stray thought from one of the aliens, something along the lines of, "He's dead all right." But Kiv was ready for the attack. He reared up on hind paws and blocked the punches. Kiv kicked with both back legs like a kangaroo. Johnny landed a few feet away before getting right back up on his feet. Kiv was still wearing the strange, sad look on his face. Johnny attacked again. The sad look disappeared, and Kiv morphed into a surprised Kiv as he blocked the punches again. He was slowly finding out that he and his human were now evenly matched. Still, Kiv had more battle experience, so he managed to sneak in another punch bad enough to send Johnny flying through the air.

And when Johnny attacked again, Kiv jumped to the side and charged from behind, disabling the mecha-suit. Johnny tumbled to the ground. As he got to his knees, he watched his hands and the tiny sparks that were now flying from thousands of tiny short circuits in his gloves. He half turned to look at Kiv, who was now back on all fours, pacing like an angry tiger.

After a long silence, the Demon chuffed and walked over to the smaller spaceships that were parked on the side of the street, like cars. He was sniffing the air as if he needed to find the scent of the human. It was hard to interpret the look on his face. Quite frankly, though, it was scary. Usually, Kiv was the monster with a stupid grin on his face.

He refused to speak, telepathically or otherwise, in front of aliens. Wouldn't stand on two legs or give any indication of intelligence. But the look on his face was scary. His emotions felt were clear. They hung in the air among the broken bottles and windows.

Johnny felt shame and more fear. Kiv simply trotted over on all fours to Johnny's small handmade spaceship, like an old wounded bloodhound. He seemed both impressed and saddened by its existence. He chuffed again and ran off, disappearing into a shocked alien crowd.

Johnny figured he'd better leave, too. And fast. The air around him was thick with questions. But first, he had to talk with Kiv. He ran into the alien crowd and followed him.

The intrepid human found his giant beast, best buddy perched on the roof of one of the buildings, staring at the moon and star-filled sky above him like some strange gargoyle.

"Hey," Johnny muttered while sitting next to Kiv. "I guess we need to talk..."

"You're going home," Kiv whispered.

"Well, I never hid that it's what I wanted."

"You have everything here, food, water. You could stay at any of our planets and choose whichever job you liked."

"Well, you have food here, too, but somehow, whenever we dock, you disappear. What's wrong? Why aren't you happy with all that?"

Something dangerous flashed in Kiv's eyes at these words, but he quickly squashed it. He heaved a deep sigh, and before long, a smile graced his features once again. It was a very sad smile. A smile no one had ever seen on Kiv. No one would have ever thought that Kiv of all monsters could smile like that.

That's when Johnny knew he had won.

"All right," mumbled Kiv.

"I guess the rules aren't fair. Let's go back home."

The flight back home was more than a little awkward. The spaceship Johnny had built was human-sized, not demon sized. And so Kiv had quite neatly folded himself and squished into the passenger seat. He seemed to be silently fuming, quiet with only constant tapping of his claws as the only clue inside his head thoughts were going ten thousand miles an hour. Johnny was worried. The only time Kiv was this quiet was when something was wrong.

But the biggest shock came when they came back to Kohutek. Once there, when they disembarked in the docking bay Kiv asked a single question:

"Is this your only spaceship, human?"

"Yes..."

"Good"

And with those words, Kiv tore Johnny's spaceship apart, piece by piece with his bare paws. As if it was nothing but a silly little toy. Claws cutting through all the materials like knives through hot butter. Methodically, silently, without much emotion. Until it was nothing but a scattered load of junk. The Demon turned and said, "You're in trouble now, human."

He was so serious, so unlike himself. With a swish of his tail, he left.

Johnny was now alone. He didn't know why his knees felt so weak. He didn't know why the next moment he was kneeling on the floor or why or where all of these sudden emotions came from. But goddammit. He felt like screaming. And so, he did.

Back on Kohutek, nobody knew where Johnny had been. Nobody knew where Kiv had been. But what everyone knew was that Kiv was peeved. And when Kiv was peeved, everybody knew to give him a wide berth. It was tense.

If Kiv would turn on Johnny, or if he ratted him out, this wasn't good. But so far, Kiv was tight lipped about their escapades. Johnny avoided him, and for his part started to hang out with Łip so much she actually started giving him knife throwing lessons.

It was during one of those lessons, the one where the lizard lady was explaining all the differences between throwing small pocket switchblades and throwing giant meat cleavers, that Johnny finally blurted out: "So how come you and your family live with the demons?" Łip paused for a second and fixed the human with a glare.

"I'm just curious. You see, you are mortal enemies. I am curious."

Łip thought a while before putting her favorite switchblade and her favorite meat cleaver on the nearest table and arranging them neatly. With her back turned, she started dejectedly, "You've been in a lizard lab: you've seen how they treat aliens. Do you really think any of us could ask those same aliens for an asylum?"

"So why the Demons then?"

"Convenience, I guess. Demons will do everything to kill off the lizard empire, and my grandparents and the great, grandparents of many others had insider knowledge." She heaved a deep sigh as if merely talking about: this caused her a great deal of pain and shame mixed together into a giant soup of sadness. A soup she was eating every day, it seemed. She turned and hugged herself as if looking for comfort.

"Not all the lizards are bad. Some are just caught in a bad system."

Before Johnny could say anything, she added, "I think you'd better leave now."

Kiv decided that the next shore leave was going to be on the Ѧ Yjakяa space station. Ѧ Yjakяa, a Young star. Everyone on the ship was shocked at this. It was Xaj'v who made such decisions.

Everyone on Kohutek knew that Kiv was second in command thanks to his fighting prowess, but Kiv had never taken the lead like this.

"This is not your decision, Kiv. I am the one to decide our next leave, not you.

Xaj'v himself looked like he was about to throw a hissy fit.

Kiv, though, would not bow.

"Xaj'v, you old bastard, you work us harder than any other captain. You should be thankful we don't mutiny." Kiv spoke in Demonese.

"Who do you think you are to challenge me, you runt?" Xaj'v shot back.

If Łip could remain calm and unperturbed when confronting the dear leader. Kiv was anything but.

"Cut the crap, you old son of a bitch. You've got no tactical skills. You have barely any foresight. The only reason why you're the leader is because you fight like hell, and you've had a hell of a lot of luck! You have run us ragged, and our supplies were dangerously close to running out on several occasions! You treat everybody like dirt. And your people skills? Don't get me started. No wonder you've only been a sperm donor; no female would want you if you treated her like you treat your crew!"

Xaj'v roared and threw himself at Kiv. Kiv jumped out of the way only to attack his brother from behind, biting and scratching like a wild animal, then pinning his opponent to the ground.

"Is this a duel, then?" Kiv laughed.

"Yes. Yes, it is!" Xaj'v seethed, his eyes like lasers.

"Well, all right then." Kiv released Xaj'v and called to Jakj'mer loud enough so everyone could hear.

"Jackie, you're my referee!" He turned back to the ship's leader. "We'll meet in the gym in half an hour!" And with that, he left.

The confusion that followed was best summed up by Kȟod when he gaped at the empty room and said, "What the fuck just happened?"

Before long, most of the Demons were gathered in the gym, waiting for the two to square off and the duel to begin. Jackie figured he'd give his human a few instructions.

"If our side loses, run like hell. Xaj'v's followers will try to rip you to shreds!"

"Well, that's reassuring. I guess?"

"Most importantly, stay out of the splash zone. There will be blood. If you get burned, Łip will have my head for not looking out for you!"

"Anything else?"

"Yes. Have fun!"

Johnny thought it looked like Jackie suspected him of something. He headed for the top of the bleachers to avoid spending any time in the so called splash zone. Demons were chuffing and snorting in excitement. The tension was palpable. Whispers hung in the air like curtains.

"I've only seen a handful of these fights. They're always a spectacle!"

"Well, I hope Xaj'v wins. He knows how to slit lizard throats like butter."

"He and Kiv are equally matched, aren't they? Damn, this is gonna be interesting!"

"You know, I've been to a fight where a rookie won, only to later die from internal injuries."

"You're kidding!"

"Nope, saw it with my own eyes. The kid wasn't even able to give a single order before he bled out."

That's when Johnny started to get nervous. Just what would happen to a loser of this particular fight? He forgot to ask, but now it began to seem like an important detail. After all, Kiv was an all-around nice guy. Yikes. Kiv was his best friend. What would happen to his best friend?

Finally, at the very top of the bleachers, Johnny found an empty seat and a relative sanctuary from the fog of whispers. On the other side of the arena on the very top of the bleachers was old J'juk'кея, who somehow managed to look interested and bored at the same time. It looked like she had crazy thoughts going through her mind that she wouldn't share.

Kiv showed up, entering the stage like an angry lion with a particularly nasty job to do. His supporters erupted in cheers and roared. Roared? If they could growl like animals, why not also roar? Walls were shaking either way.

Xaj'v entered at the same time. His back wasn't bleeding but was still raw. They were both naked as if ready they wanted to fight aliens. His followers showed their support, roaring in much the same way as Kiv's supporters.

MausӼψħ followed Xaj'v.

"Here is my referee." The current leader announced and pointed at the Demon, who may or may not have been drinking. If Jakj'mer had any trouble with this, he didn't say it. The two referees shook paws cordially.

Instantly Xaj'v threw himself at Kiv, and the fight started. It was brutal; one would never guess that they were supposed to be brothers. Xaj'v opened by grabbing his little bro's throat and trying to rip out the jugular. Kiv returned by slashing at his opponent's eyes. Those eight-inch claws missed eyes by a hair, and when they separated, both of them had chunks of skin and muscle hanging.

This was gruesome. The two opponents circled each other slowly. Kiv was so unusually quiet and cautious during this fight, unlike his behavior when fighting the lizards.

Xaj'v attacked again, and Kiv responded in kind. They fought and tumbled and wrestled. And blood was soon flying everywhere.

But other Demons? They were cheering like it was a basketball match. Why weren't the referees doing anything? Jackie and MausӼψħ seemed perfectly calm and content, and if either of them saw anything wrong, they ignored it. Neither said anything. The fight dragged on and on.

After four hours, a winner emerged when Xaj'v collapsed from pure exhaustion. Kiv didn't look much better. He was barely able to stand. He was covered in blood, head to tail, and oh yeah, one of his eyes was missing.

But the referees agreed, and Mausжψħ shouted to the crowd.

"Ladies and Gentlemen. Kohutek has a new leader!"

Jackie then finished the sentence for him.

"Kiv has won!"

CHAPTER 6

KIV'S FAMILY

The first thing that Kiv did as the newly installed leader was to visit the Med Bay, where Łip in her beloved hazmat suit was now patching up both of the contestants. She was quiet for a while, but this time, unlike J'juk'кея, she wasn't afraid to voice her thoughts out loud.

"So, you're the boss now? Huh? Have you got any kids yet?"

"Let me guess. I broke the law?" Kiv was somewhat bemused.

"No, but you're awfully close to losing the apparatus. If you were to die childless, then..."

"Then, the elders won't have any fresh meat to mold into soldiers."

Ł'łяояа heaved a long-suffering sigh. Johnny was sitting cross-legged on a nearby gurney watching as the medic patched up Kiv's wounds.

"You know what bugs me the most?" Kiv started. "I could have my eye replaced."

"Here, we go again." Ł'łяояа rolled her eyes.

"I'm not just being petty. I know ladies like battle scars: I just want to see where I'm going!" Kiv kept ranting.

"Well, I don't make those laws." Ł'łяояа countered. "And if you try to change them by challenging the elders of all people, you'll find hell like no other." She was now was at the stage of sewing together the eyelids over the empty eye socket.

"This is getting dangerous, Kiv." She admonished him harshly.

"Your family will face the consequences if you die with no offspring."

Kiv tensed at those words. There was something that wasn't being said.

Ł'łяояа was never one to give up easily, even if faced with a losing battle.

"You know about G'juat don't you?"

"G'juat's into robots, so what? They make a great friend." Kiv was now getting defensive.

"G'juat is also from one of the most in-bred families of ours. He has lost several children now. And with your genes..."

"I'm no breeding bull."

"But you never let anyone, female or otherwise, get close to you! And then you dare to give hell to your brother for doing what's expected of him! What other option is there?"

"They won't see me! They'll see my genes. Just my genes, that's all!"

Ł'łяояа could be quick to anger sometimes, but she was also quick to calm down.

"Listen, Kiv. You. You are the leader now. There are certain things expected of you now." She swallowed quietly before continuing. "You want us to fly back to A Yjakяа. Fine, awesome, but how do you think the elders there will react? Would you at least try to pretend you're following the law? Otherwise, your stint as a leader will be short lived."

And with that, she left.

So now they arrived at A Yjakяа. Finally! A Yjakяа was a space base on the biggest planet near the center of the galaxy. It was full of robots and empty spaces. Demons numbered only one billion, so their planet space station was mostly empty, save for the three billion very happy robots. Demons filled up the vacant spaces with statues of their most famous warriors. From the information engraved next to those statues, Johnny gathered that apparently, in order to be recognized as a hero by the Demons, you had to be... kind of...dead...Huh...Figures.

As far as statues go, some were tall, some were small. Some didn't look like anything at all. But all seemed unforgettable with a strange metallic shine to them, unlike anything found on Earth - each with a small bejeweled sign spelling out the name and deeds of the commemorated individual.

There were statues for the accomplished robots and the statue for a philosopher robot, and a few explorer robots who had their own sculptures. There was even a statue of a robot janitor who evacuated a whole planet when it was about to be destroyed by a meteor.

G'juat was now going to leave on his extended vacation, and hugs were exchanged with the rest of the crew. Johnny was still hugging G'juat when Kiv grabbed him by the shoulder.

"You're coming with me," the monster hissed; he dragged Johnny past a few of the gaudiest of the tacky statues, one depicting a Demon in the middle of devouring a lizard. Another statue had some demon striking the "I'm a lion roaring at midnight" pose. And statue figure of a robot, what, plumber? Okay, how did he get up there? Nope, no time to stop and look; Kiv was on a mission.

Kiv dragged Johnny through oddly narrow streets, across courtyards, and into unmarked alleys. It seemed that they were entering one of the more impoverished neighborhoods of A Yjakяa.

Kiv kicked open the doors to a rundown building; to their right were windows with a lovely view of the galaxy and to the left a row of doors leading to apartments. Sometimes those doors were broken, missing, and never replaced. Johnny peeked in to see piles of trash as well as puddles of god-knows-what that turned the floors into a scary looking mess. The robots that living in this area were old and rusty. Kiv gave Johnny a sideways glance out of his one good eye left and finally asked the question that hung between them.

"You've heard how I was made, right?"

Johnny nodded mutely.

"Good," Kiv replied.

"We're almost there." They turned a corner and arrived as only what could be described as two or three apartments connected together to make one large apartment suitable for a larger family. One of the doors was barricaded entirely, while the other was just an old-fashioned rusted gate that looked like it was stolen from someone's garden. It hung haphazardly in its frame and looked like it was about to fall. Kiv didn't need to knock, though. There was a small baby demon standing nearby who recognized him and immediately shouted,

"Big brother's back!"

"Big brother's back!" Soon a few Demon faces and their robot caretakers peeked around:

"Kiv's back!"

"He's back!"

"Finally! We waited so long!"

Kiv's family was big. Really big. There were a hundred of them, all spilling out the doors, hanging out the windows, all happy to see their brother. Soon they engulfed him in a giant group hug.

Yet Johnny couldn't help notice that Kiv seemed to be older than nearly all of them.

The family reunion was not over yet, and the little treasures soon turned their attention to the hapless human and started playing the hundred questions game:

"Are you really a human?"

"Do you like Demons?"

"How did you get here?"

It would have been nice if they didn't all try to out-shout each other, but at least they all knew how to speak English. Kiv attempted to rein them all in with a thunderous "Hey!" that was louder than necessary. Or so it would have seemed. The kids did calm down. Only for a moment until the rowdy bunch of a hundred baby monsters surrounded them and dragged them into the already too small space of their apartment.

The rooms smelled like ten thousand dirty socks and too many air fresheners. The place had crazy energy about it. Robots who took care of the monster litter were shabby looking but seemed happy to be a part of the family. And Kiv introduced them to his human.

"This is Auntie Xip, still in love with everything that's alive. That's my little sis Mev, my other sister Ξąv, and here's my brother Ŧav. Here are our uncles, Jip and Źip, and here's another brother of mine Kąv. He'll be joining the army soon."

All in all, it seemed there were about a hundred little monsters and their robot nannies crammed in the tiny space. The robots and some older siblings brought food in. There was hardly enough of it to go around, but it was served with joy and pride, and no one dared to refuse it. There were jokes and laughter, and after the meal, old-fashioned board games.

The evening passed happily in the warmth of the big family. Night came, and Johnny was offered a comfortable spot to sleep on the floor. The beds were all taken by little monsters. There were three to four of those boisterous little critters to each bed. For his part, Kiv was sleeping on the Kitchen table.

Johnny tossed and turned and couldn't sleep. It wasn't the hushed whispers and laughs of those little demons who refused to sleep despite the late hour. It wasn't the quiet snores of little souls fast asleep.

Johnny finally figured that maybe a glass of water would help with his restlessness. The robots all sat powered down in the chairs. The small kitchen was rustic-looking. The furniture was falling apart and held together with duct tape; the oven was modern but also held together with duct tape. The fridge seemed like the newest addition. And oh, hello, duct-taped too, my old friend. He wondered what happened to the fridge door, exactly?

And what was it that Johnny was searching for, anyways? Oh, right. Water. Johnny soon found himself a glass and filled it with something to drink. Kiv was snoring gently on the table. Bemused, Johnny looked again at the oven and noticed that there was a datapad lying on top.

Probably someone should take it away before it could get baked to a crisp. Johnny took it and looked around to see if he could find any other safe space to lay it down. The kitchen counters were drowning in dishes and unfinished food, so were the cupboards. The dishwasher was on, working overtime, but it didn't change the fact that there were dishes on top of it, too. Kiv was still asleep on the table. Maybe when he woke up, he'd want to read something?

Johnny turned on the datapad to see what was actually on it. And what was on it? Mostly newspaper articles. With nothing else to do, Johnny figured he'd read the articles.

Titles like "Disgraced crazy scientist and his brood," "From hero to zero," and "The great fifty. What happens now?" Johnny was picking up some kind of trend. Intrigued, he spent the next few hours reading the articles. Those articles, one by one, chased any semblance of sleep from our human's mind.

These articles seemed to document the rise and fall of a Demon scientist, inbred and ugly and declared unfit for combat. The only remarkable thing he did have was a brilliant mind. His name was Hӕśhяa, a name that meant 'a mistake that makes the whole perfect' or 'one who teaches a valuable lesson.' How fitting.

Hӕśhяa had done a few experiments, all dealing with effects of inbreeding, avoiding the genetic bottle-necking, and creating and re-creating genetic variety in a species. His passions led him to create genetically modified infant demons genetically unrelated to any other Demon in their galaxy. In other words, those babies were the Demon version of living gold; their genetic material was in high demand. He didn't give his children real names. He just numbered them. Half of them died because their new genes were incompatible with the original ones and had made sustainable life impossible. Other demons tolerated Hӕśhяa and these shenanigans, but barely, and only because they knew how close their species was to extinction.

But then disaster struck. The demons discovered that some of the genetic material Hӕśhяa used had come from their undesirable alien neighbors and not from the mutant animals from one of their own planets. Whether these genes came from cadavers or from illegal trade didn't matter. Usually, Demons tolerated genetic splicing on the condition these genes only come from the lizards that came to support their side.

Whatever alibi Hжśħяa had didn't matter. His peers simply needed an excuse to rip him to shreds. And that's precisely what they did. All was left of Hжśħяa were his broken bones. He was survived by his 50 genetically modified kids, who, although not sentenced to death, were left to live in a small apartment. Having read all this, Johnny came back to the living room, navigating between bunk beds and hammocks, and sat down back on the floor. He crawled underneath his blanket near his pillow. He wasn't going to sleep that night.

When morning came, such as it could be called on a space station, Kiv wandered in half-drunk from sleep. He took one look at the datapad and another he cast on the human.

"So now you know," was all he said.

CHAPTER 7

THE BIGGEST FIGHT

Over the next few days, life was rather dull and sweet. But Johnny couldn't stop thinking about things. There was a change hanging in the air, and a change slowly forming in the human's heart. What kind of change? Johnny wasn't sure, but it seemed like a significant kind of change. Change as confident as a supernova of a giant old dying star.

Kiv seemed resigned to answer all the stupid questions. At least he tried to. Unlike J'juk'keя, Kiv's patience had limits.

"Don't you think that the war should end?"

"Maybe, but I'm not going to end it."

"Don't you think if we killed the Lizard King, the war would end?"

"No, you human nitwit. That would create a power vacuum and make things worse."

"But then you could open your bor..."

"No, we couldn't. We're like the garbage men of the galaxies. We are tolerated because we do an essential task, but we have to pretend that we don't exist."

"But..."

"There are no "buts" here, human!"

Johnny decided then and there that he would have to leave before the argument got too far out of control. If he didn't, Kiv would go. And so, more often than not, Johnny left and wandered aimlessly through the halls and squares of Ꙝ Yjakяa. Turning a corner from the courtyard into an alley, he walked straight into J'juk'keя herself. In a shabby and half abandoned hallway, she stood underneath a leaking pipe, looking out the window at the stars. Like the queen of silence as she was, she greeted the approaching human with the same silence as was always her way.

She gave him one pointed look before saying, "You know about Kiv." A statement, not a question.

"Yes."

"You are trying to persuade him to do something crazy."

"Yes."

J'juk'keя was silent for a second or two. When she finally decided to say something, it was spoken softly and deliberately.

"You know that's all we know, war. Without it, what will we do?" And with that, she left.

Well, that was strange, Johnny thought, but typical of J'juk'keя. Since the situation was such that Kiv still had his secrets, and he still didn't like to talk about them much, the "intrepid human" decided to go sightseeing.

The spaceship planet opened up her gates and greeted the strange little tourist with coldness and indifference. There were more than a few shopping malls and shopping halls and plenty of empty spaces where the stores were supposed to be but were left vacant for some reason. The whole of A Yjakяa looked very modern, and half finished. The robots seemed happy. Then again, the robots were always happy.

When Johnny asked what was there to do in their free time, more than a few helpful robots gave directions to the nearest amusement parks as well as a multitude of museums. When it came to amusement parks, Johnny left each and every one of them after five minutes. It wasn't that the rides were miserable or dangerous. Rather, it was that the parks were just like most of A Yjakяa. Mostly empty and resembling ghost towns.

The museums were not much better. A new exhibit by Jip, an extremely talented and respected artist, was in town. The museum had an amazing crowd of about thirty-five guests.

At this point, Johnny was sure that Kiv and his family made up a quarter of the planet's inhabitants. That was the only logical explanation!

Frustrated, Johnny decided to walk over to the nearest wall and bang his head against it. A concerned museum guard came to him and asked what he was doing. Johnny complained that this place was incredibly empty. A few more explanations and the guard had an idea.

"Why don't you go to the zoo, then? There's always a big crowd there, my friend."

And so, Johnny went off to see whatever he could at the zoo. It was a thing that the monsters would call a zoo. To start, it was a series of cages with giant screens displaying an artist's renditions of what the natural environment for each animal was supposed to be. But then there were the animals themselves.

Ants and a giant array of bugs. All right, all good there.

Next up were the fishes - same old, same old.

The cute little frogs and salamanders. Interesting.

But next was what came as the first shock. Next to the frogs were bald mice modified genetically to display the same array of colors and produce the same toxins as the frogs. This wasn't scary.

It was about to get worse.

Next to them were mice modified to grow spikes; others had mandibles like those found in ants that seemed to be grafted on.

Johnny ran straight into to the next exhibit, and he found himself surrounded by mammals. Dogs, pigs, and a happy robot zoo keeper humming to himself while cleaning the cages.

A melancholy pod of dolphins swam in endless circles in a tank to his right. Those poor creatures had never seen a sky above their heads.

Everything there felt wrong. The animals were gone. Mindless, soulless. Empty. They couldn't even notice a strange lost human.

Johnny didn't know why but started weeping at sight. He felt like one of those crazy dolphins. But things didn't end here. No, they were about to get worse. From a nearby tank, he heard strange barking. He followed this sound despite himself. He suspected what it meant, but it didn't lessen the shock.

In the other tank, dogs looked like golden retrievers or Labradors—genetically enhanced Labradors, modified to resemble, oh no, sea lions.

Yup, according to the information engraved on a small plaque, the original sea lion DNA was lost somewhere in space. Demons used whatever creatures were available to re-create and approximate the animals for "the pleasure and amusement of our esteemed guests."

Johnny had had enough. He stormed out of the zoo, heartbroken and angry, feeling like he was about to go nuts.

So here we go, Johnny thought. I'll have to talk to Kiv again. Persuade him to end this war. Kill the Lizard king. How would that go?

Not well. Kiv threw a fit. So, was it going to be a fight? Yes, indeed.

It became one hell of a fight. Johnny had never seen Kiv so angry. He had never been as angry himself. He was equally angry and scared. He ran to get his mecha-suit while avoiding the punches and kicks and bites of his friend turned leader.

"I protected you!" Kiv screamed before literally climbing up a wall.

"I kept you safe!" The monster did a somersault and landed in front of Johnny.

"And you still want to disobey us." Kiv snarled like a rabid animal while Johnny did his best to slip past the furious beast.

"You ungrateful child! Son of a bitch! You think you know how to win this war? If it was that easy, we would have killed the Lizard king a long time ago! What you suggest is nothing but a suicide mission!"

Things were getting out of hand and fast. Johnny was pretty sure that he was about to die. At the last moment, help came from an unlikely angel, or more precisely from one very grumpy old space fairy godmother.

J'juk'keя, being very unlike J'juk'keя appeared out of nowhere and stood eye-to-eye with Kiv, turning her ire directly toward him. She had no intention of lecturing the little human.

"You're condemning him to death." she barked at the other monster in Demonese.

"I'm protecting him."

"But sooner or later, he'll go home. Don't think you can stop him. And then what?"

J'juk'keя stood up on her hind legs and turned sideways to show off the side of her body that looked like it was melted and then regrown again.

"You will end up like me." J'juk'keя was calm yet serious, deadly serious.

Kiv wanted to start to argue again, but old J'juk'keя roared before he could even open his mouth. Yes. She roared, roared like a lioness queen that she was. (Important side notes: if demons' growl could cause the walls to shake, their roar could easily damage your eardrums.) For Johnny, the deafness was temporary, and when his hearing returned, he could finally catch the rest of J'juk'keя's angry lecture.

"Your crew will turn on you," she snarled again, moving closer to Kiv. "They will turn on you like they turned on me."

She was a breath away now.

"They will rip you apart like they ripped me to shreds all those decades ago!" And you will become what I am now." She continued with her hellish sermon.

Kiv's anger was gone, replaced by fear. Meekly he said:

"But the human. He says we should just kill the Lizard king. It's impossible."

"Is it really impossible?" J'juk'кея answered calmly, "Or are you just afraid that once the lizards are defeated, we won't have our place in this galaxy anymore?"

And that's how Kiv backed down. And Johnny knew that he would kill the Lizard king.

They started to make plans. They were getting ready to cripple and destroy the lizards once and for all.

CHAPTER 8

THE END

The reptile mothership was the size of a planet. It wasn't a planet, though. It was too clean and too orderly to be one. It seemed that any life that could have started naturally on an ordinary planet at any point in time was, in fact, methodically disinfected into oblivion by the tired and underpaid lizard janitors. It was beautiful in a way; all it needed was an original and ominous orchestral score.

Of course, sneaking on to this mothership, it was easier said than done. Other Aliens stayed away from that damned, godforsaken thing.

Who could blame them? On average internal organs tend to work better inside the body. And Lizards tended to disagree with that opinion.

It was impossible to teleport into the ship. And why? This thing was protected by a force field. How would they get in?

J'juk'keя smiled. She had an idea. "Stowaway on one of the smaller Lizard ships and get in that way."

"Will it work?"

"Maybe. Everyone gives them a wide berth. They probably won't even suspect that anyone would try to sneak in on one of their own ships while they are away on another planet."

"And if they find us?"

"Then, they kill us."

That made sense. What made less sense was the fact that J'juk'keя was going with them. When asked about this, she simply said, "I've got nothing better to do."

The details of getting on the small cargo lizard ship weren't complicated. While the lizards stopped at a small alien planet to drink enough alcohol to drown an elephant, Johnny used his knowledge of all the classic Hollywood movies to sneak onto and hide aboard their ship.

And it worked! He couldn't believe it. J'juk'keя and Kiv didn't believe it either.

Kiv, of course, had to comment on the matter. "I don't care if we're about to die. Don't you ever make me wear a pink tutu again!"

Well, to be honest, it wasn't necessary, but it sure was funny! At least as far as Johnny was concerned.

J'juk'keя, as always, suffered in silence.

And then they waited. And waited. What happened? Absolutely nothing. Before going back to the mothership, the lizards had to fill in paperwork - easy digital paperwork but paperwork none the less. The bureaucracy had its evil powers stretching into the farthest reaches of the universe.

The lizard's craft launched and returned to the mothership, landing smoothly. The pilots never noticed the extra cargo that Johnny, Kiv, and J'juk'keя added to their ballast.

The three stowaways waited a long time before for the hangar emptied of most of the lizards and before the ever-watchful eyes of the circulating cameras turned elsewhere. And after that?

They moved to the best option for moving through the ship. The ventilation shafts? No, that would be too easy. Not the ventilation shaft but a ship's sewer lines. The smell of ammonia was so bad, Johnny nearly puked.

"Don't worry," Kiv laughed. "You'll get used to it after a couple of days."

"DAYS???!!!"

"Well, yes," J'juk'keя explained patiently. "This is the mother ship. It's the size of a planet."

A couple of days later, and the smell really did stop bothering our intrepid human. He definitely loved the fact that he had managed to bring a mecha-suit with him. He would not be able to keep up with his demon friends without it. What he couldn't get used to was Kiv almost drowning in a literal river of excrement. While Kiv was clowning around doing his usual doofus routine, he slipped and fell and disappeared into the muck below.

"Don't just stand there! Help him, J'juk'keя!"

"I can't. Our bones are eight times denser than yours. We sink."

Johnny was getting ready to jump in when Kiv burst through the surface and crawled onto the edge like a muddy walrus. Without a word, J'juk'keя emptied her water pouch to wash the sludge from Kiv's eyes.

"How are you still alive? You sank!"

"I can close and open my nostrils like a whale does. I walked through the bottom of the river and climbed out onto the edge, and here I am."

Their journey continued, and more days passed. Why, oh why, must everything in life be so dark and boring? Still, there were times where he could look up through the grates and see a Lizard lab, the same kind in which he once was a prisoner. He felt certain nausea at the scenes, nausea that had nothing to do with the ever present stench.

"Shouldn't we save them?" he asked.

Both demons replied with a firm, deadpan, "No."

"But isn't it what you guys do?" insisted Johnny. "You're the heroes of the galaxy. Doesn't everyone applaud you for killing the lizards and saving all the aliens?"

Kiv chuckled at this statement.

"Kid, we don't save them; we free them. Then they make up stories! But this time, we have a mission."

And so, they continued on. The lights through sewer grates showed lab after lab. And the light shining through them kept bringing some more horrific images into view. Aliens in cages. Aliens on examination tables. Aliens in varying states of dissection. Johnny had to try again.

"But if we freed them all at the same time, wouldn't the confusion help us?"

"If we freed them, they'd be dead," J'juk'кея replied with some exasperation.

"She's right," Kiv added, "They have poison gas; they can pump into the chambers at any time."

"But..."

"We don't just go berserk whenever we attack a Lizard ship. We always have a plan. We damage the controls enough so that they can't push the button and gas us all. But here? There are only three of us! We're outnumbered; we have to be careful. We don't want to just alert the command and the Lizard king that there's some infestation on the ship!"

"But they're dying!"

Kiv sighed deeply upon hearing this. He turned to J'juk'keя and said in the demon language, "Maybe we should switch to some faster method of travel. Otherwise, he won't stop nagging us about this."

"We'll need a trip to the spa first," J'juk'keя muttered.

So, they took out their datapads and looked at the maps and schematics of the mothership contained within. An app for navigating this mothership was a handy addition. It led them to a place where a sewer wall bordered the elevator shaft.

"Ready?" asked Kiv. Oh yeah, they were ready. All three of them literally punched holes with their fists until they created an opening where all three could fit. As soon as the first elevator stopped at the floor going down, they jumped on it and attached themselves to its roof. The lizards inside had no clue. And the elevator did go much faster. They hung on tight as the elevator sped downward. The three held on as the elevator descended and kept completely silent. And they just kept falling and falling. It seemed like forever, down the rabbit hole like some messed up version of **Alice in Wonderland**. Finally, the elevator gradually slowed to a stop.

"Are we there yet?" Asked Johnny.

"No," replied J'juk'keя, checking while staring at her datapad.

The elevator then started going down again, and again, it felt like an eternity. And when it stopped:

"Are we there..."

"Nope"

"H... How many... hours?"

"Six."

And the elevator started moving again. And off they went again. And since there was nothing to do, Johnny figured that he might as well admire the architecture inside the lizard elevator shaft. Very utilitarian, and very dull and windy. And the silence was so awkward our human figured he should probably talk about something else now.

"So. Once we kill that Lizard king, are you going to go and write a book or something?"

J'juk'keя responded by fixing on him with her patented, "you are stupid" glare. Seriously though, why did he even flinch? It was a general law of the universe that J'juk'keя would stare at someone as if they were stupid at least five times a day, every day. Same as e=mc2 and other such things.

"Well, you know, if I kill the Lizard King, I know what I'll do. I'll fly home. but I was just wondering what..."

"Heh! I'll make life easy for you," Kiv butted in. "We'll go with ya and visit Earth!"

Well, this was new. How come his overgrown neon mutants never told him that before?

Kiv shrugged and gave his impish smile. "You think that our people will be grateful that we've destroyed their life's purpose?" Kiv looked at Johnny, his eyes turning serious for once, his smile tight.

"When the evil Lizard king and his empire is gone, the one job we're all good at will disappear as well. And you really think that we'll be seen as heroes? Let's not even mention other aliens. They don't really love us; they tolerate us. Without the lizards, they will have other ideas about us."

"Quit whining," J'juk'keя snapped. "What probably will happen is that we'll discover that our people are worked up over nothing. The aliens have laws, but they have hearts too. They'll know we had no choice, that they owe us their lives. Our people will be safe. Me? I just want to go to Earth just to relax and finally retire."

"What about your family then?" Johnny asked. He instantly regretted it since Kiv immediately sobered up when he heard it.

"They'll be fine," he muttered.

"Yep, we're here," J'juk'keя announced as casually as she'd speak to her grandchildren. The maps on the datapad showed them where to break into the sewer again. It was more challenging this time. They were so tired.

They found a dry place on the edge of the sewer line to curl up for some sleep. J'juk'keя watched over them like a granny.

A few hours later, J'juk'keя woke them gently.

"We're close to royal chambers."

They were finally able to leave the sewer, and they could sneak through the hallways. They had to take out all the guards along the way because their smell was so bad, they couldn't sneak past them. The plan was the same. Destroy the security cameras and then the guards. Preferably in that order.

The first one was easy. J'juk'keя took out her datapad, and what do you know. Demons also had apps for hacking and disabling security systems.

Now for the next part of the plan.

"I want to thank you, Johnny" Kiv turned to him.

"Oh? What for?" The intrepid human had no clue.

"For volunteering as bait." Kiv pushed his helpless pet right around the corner and in front of the guards. Mecha-suit or not, Johnny was not going to fight all fifteen guards at once. Lucky for him, the guards had never seen a human in a mecha-suit in the middle of their spaceship. They just stood there open-mouthed, staring at him.

"H...Hi." Johnny waved at them sheepishly, and the spell was broken. With their plasma guns ready, the snarling monster lizards started chasing him. When those guards ran past Kiv and J'juk'keя, the two picked them off one by one until none were left. And that was that.

Kiv led them through the corridor into the royal lizard chambers. The old King sat on his throne in a giant empty chamber reading on his favorite datapad.

"Who's there?" The King called out telepathically and knew immediately what the silence meant. Johnny shrugged; he almost forgot that telepathy was the international language of the aliens.

The energy changed. Johnny could sense only danger. The King stood from his throne, and he took one look at his guests.

"Are you here to kill me?"

"Yes."

"Go ahead, then."

With that, they killed the Lizard king. It was too easy and weirdly anticlimactic.

The three stood over the corpse and saluted each other. But before they could consider an escape, there would be a forest of lizards to cut through.

The King's army charged into the throne room, telepathically called in by the Lizard King's last thoughts. They took one look at the dead monarch and the ones who stood above his corpse. The epic battle began.

Back to back, Kiv and Johnny, in his mecha-suit, grabbed the lizard's plasma guns and sprayed fire across the nearest lizards, dodging fire as they moved to cover in the throne room.

J'juk'keя had disappeared, and Kiv and Johnny hardly noticed while they were trying to stay alive.

As they skirted the edge of the room, she tossed them something: a bundle, a flexible woven metal blanket.

"Quick. Cover up!"

She had slid under the Lizard soldiers' throne and retrieved what she suspected would be there behind the throne. She dove under Kiv's draped blanket and deftly entered the code on her datapad.

The hiss of the gasses sent all the lizards into a panic. They ran for the doors and into hallways, already blocked by others sinking to the floor.

Johnny whispered to himself. "What is happening?"

Johnny felt a kick from outside his cover. The scraping of the metal fabric matched the sound of Johnny's own cover.

"You still with us?" Kiv's voice was muffled by the coverings but was reason enough for both Johnny to finally take a breath.

"The poisoned gas. I was saving it for something just like this." J'juk'кея said as she pushed on the mecha-suit under the weighted cover. "This works like a gas mask. We should be OK while the lizards all collapse." She kicked Johnny's mecha-suit again. "I always have a plan."

And so, we come to the end of this story.

Our heroes returned home with stories and rumors flying wildly about them. The truth was out. Soon the entire galaxy would know about it. The lizards were dead. The aliens, all released from their cages in the airlocked labs, ambushed their captors there and waited for the gasses outside the labs to clear.

Kiv was now banished from his own people, and Johnny was free to go home to his family. Really, the Demon laws are insanely confusing, Johnny thought. Kiv had done the impossible, and now he was banished?

"I'll have to ask J'juk'кея about it someday."

As for J'juk'кея, she was also banished. Twice now. Either that or she just didn't give a damn about a society that had rejected her.

As they packed up to leave, Johnny led them to a long-forgotten spaceship he had retrofitted months ago for a long, long trip to Earth.

"Are you two coming?"

Kiv and J'juk'кея both nodded. With hardly a look back, the three launched the stolen spaceship into the dark emptiness outside their planet.

"So, do you think we can maybe pick up about a hundred of my younger siblings and bring them over to earth for a little vacation?"

"What?!" Johnny sputtered, "you couldn't have told me this earlier? I would have stolen a bigger ship!"

"Whatever." J'juk'кея grumbled.

THE END